IN TWO PARTS

HIEROGLYPHS / PRIMA FACIE

Selected Poetry and Short fiction

By

Edward D. Currelley

PUBLISHED BY PEN TO MIND BOOKS

Copyright © 2024 by Edward D. Currelley

For more information, or to book an event, contact :

pentomindbooks@gmail.com

edwardcurrelley@gmail.com

Cover design by : Kelly Preusser

Kelly@greyprinting.com

Editor : C. Layne

Produced by : Niamani Inks

Empress.Poetry1@gmail.com

ISBN : 979-8-218-47909-1

First Edition : July 2024

Pen to Mind Books
since 2014

CONTENTS: HIEROGLYPHS / Poetry

Stories Told in Silence
Change is coming
High Stakes Gamble
Mud Scrolls
The Skin That I'm In

CONTENTS: PRIMA FACIE

PUBLISHING: ACKNOWLEDGMENTS

Grateful acknowledgment is made to the following publications in which some of these poems and stories first appeared.

POETRY

Nature's Song
Published 2015: Writing for Peace, Dove Tales "Nature"
Published 2015:
"Love Thy Neighbor" Online
Published 2016: Poetry
Nation

Wait We
Published 2016: Indent Books, "HIV HERE and NOW
PROJECT" – Online

I America
Published 2017: Split This Rock, "Poems of
Resistance, Power & Resilience" – Online
Published 2017: Dove Tales, "Refugees and the
Displaced"

Silver
Published 2015: MER (Mom Egg Review) VOX Gallery,
"Selections on age/aging" – Online.

Everyday Adventure
Published 2014: Eber & Wein, "Across the Way
Mountain"
Published 2022: National beat Poetry Foundation, "New
Generation Beats."

Magical Mornings at the Gazebo
Published 2016: Metaphor, Issue # 5

My Mother's War
Published 2015: Mom Egg Review, "Issue #13"

MUD Scrolls
Published 2017: HVCCA "Between I & Thou" Writing the
Walls

Perfection / Reflection – Strength & Fragility
Published 2018: HVCCA – "Death is Irrelevant" Writing
the Walls

Tom Boy
Published 2022: International Beat Poetry Foundation,
"Goddess Anthology"

Insatiable Intoxication
Published 2022: National Beat Poetry Foundation,
"Remembering Jack Kerouac"

Heartfelt Connection
Published 2023: HVCCA – "Between the Eye of the
Needle"
Writing the Walls

Short Stories

Dark Perspectives
Published 2018: Writing for Peace, Dove Tales,
"Empathy in Art - Embracing the Other"

Sacrifice Paid Forward
Published 2019: Writing for Peace, Dove Tales, "One
World - One People"

Fractured Soul
Published 2016: Writing for Peace, Dove Tales, "Family
& Cultural Identity"

FORWARD

Hieroglyphs / Prima Facie is a compilation of poems and short fiction, two books in one, universal observations. Topics included are love, strength, environment, politics, human interest, sentimentality, and nature. The works were created for reflection, acknowledgment of our differences and right of existence in all facets of life, to explore an empathetic path to understanding. To inspire and more importantly for the reader to understand our personal stake and appreciation for the planet and humanity, our survival, and the limited time we have here individually and collectively, our need to assist in its preservation on a multitude of levels for generations to come. What we do now and leave behind will be the legacy of the human species if anything is left at all.

DEDICATIONS

There are so many people to thank. I cannot single out everyone individually. My heartfelt gratitude and appreciation go out to all, respectively. There are, however, four people whom I must single out. Without their individual love and support this book may never have been possible. First being my mother, Annie Daniels Currelley. I am the sixth of seven children. Being a single mom for most of our lives, she somehow managed to nurture into blossom her children's creative and all inspired interest. There are so many wonderful memories. She was everything to us. Though, she's been gone for many years. Her presence is continually felt throughout our daily lives. I know she is looking down and smiling proudly at her children utilizing the tools of life she provided and the gifts from God she encouraged.

My life and all that I am, accomplishments and achievements fail in comparison to this woman who set me on my path. This book, these words; are a monument to the wonderful person she was. The good her children do and the people they have become is testimony to the legacy she leaves behind.
Second, my sister Lorraine Currelley, we've dreamed on long walks in youth and continue dreaming to this day. You have always been there and continue to be here for me. No words can express my gratitude and appreciation for all the support and encouragement you have so generously given, thank you. Third, my sister Janice Nahshal whose warm wishes and kind blessings of encouragement have carried me through numerous bouts of doubt and indecision, thank you.

Last, Serena, my friend and life partner for more than twenty-five years. We have held hands during each of our darkest and brightest periods and survived against unthinkable odds. Thank you for all your warmth, support, and encouragement.

IN TWO PARTS

HIEROGLYPHS / PRIMA FACIE

Selected Poetry and Short fiction

HIEROGLYPHS

A look at who we are, what we mean. Our legacy of humanity contribution of continuance, stewardship of planet and evidence of existence

LOVE

SERENA SMILE

Your lips
That smile
The place behind your eyes that always question
Pondering the source of our love
Years of companionship, friendship
Still, I am captivated by your beauty and warmth
That steadfast notion of what life should be; could be
The constant exploration of true purpose
The feeling of holding hands
Walking an un-charted path
Heart to heart
Without expectation
Together
Just being together
You me, being us
Just being us

PEACEFUL COMFORT

We lay silently
Your body pressed against mine
The warmth of your breath upon my spine
You curl around me to become one
The magnificence of nature part in offering
Expectation and anticipation overwhelming
My breath traces the contours of your innocence
I languish at the glistening reflection of your joy
I feast upon the nectar of our love
The sensation of fulfillment overtakes me
Our eyes tear
Filled with contentment
We lay silent
The joy of knowing peaceful comfort
We hold and curl
Still, like spoons lined in a drawer
Your heart beats calmly
I sigh, you exhale, and all is well

BLOOD IN KIND

Blood of mine that flow through those in kind
We chant the mantra of family
Them that say blood is thicker than water
Yet, spill it in self-serving moments of convenience
Apologies demanded to ease the pain of self-inflicted wounds
Red waters flowing like a stream rising above the banks
Spilled blood does not mop away without trace
Assumed love is no guarantee of forgiveness
Shared blood is not a protection against the consequence of action
The blood of mine that feel the pain in kind is loved
Wounds mend, time heals, blood flows and life continues

SILVER

I lay awake
Thoughts of you, of times past
The sound of your footsteps pacing
The sanctuary of hot coffee
Silver of your hair glistening under a single kitchen bulb
Silver the age of restless
Awakened long before dawn
Silver doesn't need much sleep
I ponder your thoughts
Away in the unfamiliar
Surrounded by darkness
Praying for sunshine
Fear of the un-known
Confused, frustration
My wide-eyed doe
In the middle of traffic
Stumbling in the rain
Heart pounding
Seeking peace, comfort, freedom
Hoping, praying that the next set of head lights belong to the familiar
And comes to a screeching halt

HEARTFELT CONNECTION

Last night my dreams were about you
Yes dreams, plural
Always in multiples of three
Deep love
Fanciful flirtations of love
Dreaded ending of love
I've tarried in quest to understand deep love
The attachment, unyielding bond
To reason why we cry for one another
Clash, find minds at odds
While hearts remain fixed
Feels like ill-gotten gain
At moment of forgiveness
Fanciful flirtation from across the room
Your gaze, small wrinkle in your cheek
Squinting crow's feet, accompanied by a smile
The curious arched brow
Fingertip pointing to the crease in your chin
That mischievous grin
The age of golden, shining brightly in your eyes
Intertwined fingers and gentle kisses
The unspeakable dreaded end, arriving much too soon
Physical separation a farce
The heart is strong
Realization we are no more, yet will always be
Constant examination of reasoning for loss
While connection remains
Absence of warmth, the crave for tenderness
The fading of togetherness
Scent of forgotten garments
Sleeping on your side of the bed
Dreaming of eternal love in plural
Listening to the heart of one that now beats for two

Grateful for tearful eyes, joyful feelings, and memories that will always remain

THERE BE MONSTER AND DRAGONS

Free spirited
Un-bridled, wild child
Connection clear, un-defined roles of lost souls
Boundaries crossed friendships lost
The wrath of infidelity strikes hard
Fine dine, great wine
Art treasures of passion, naked souls abound
Masks that fool no one
Thursday night drunken flight
Hotel, Botel, Grove, or the Pines
Monday red eye, blind to the shine
Sand or concrete, couldn't tell the difference
The road home from oblivion is never clear
Never cheap, and never hidden
All that is revealed in darkness
Will eventually find its way to the light

NURTURING CHANGE

Took your presence for granted
Never imagined the vacancy that came to soon
The hole in my heart, a bottomless pit
A void that was Mandela's reality
You forced change into my life
Unwelcomed at the time
With it, came strength and independence
I miss being held by you
Comforted during times of weakness
Times when I felt so alone, heart breaking
The adult child in need of nurturing
Mother's affection, mother's love
Being different hurt so bad
My tears over flowed
You smiled, without judgment, understanding fully
The world has changed in your absence
It continues to move forward at an astonishing rate
It cannot be stopped or slowed down
Your kindness, love respect for all that lives
Is being paid forward, endlessly
The pain of change has not stopped
Mending the wounds of the fractured
Tending the souls of loneliness
Continue with compassion

SAY SOMETHING SWEET

Ouch! Don't grab
You're not picking fruit
Take it out, but not on me
For once, can you be gentle
Maybe even, say something sweet
Leave your day at the door, along with your boots
Hang your attitude in the closet as I do
Before you get home
Put all to rest, as I do the children
So, our night will be calm
Hold me gently, caress me
Say something sweet
Say the things that I need to hear
The warm whispers of love that touch me, inside
Deeper than you will ever penetrate
Those places that are, sacred
The dark hollows of my mind, my soul, my heart
Say something sweet
So, I am willing and wanting to comfort

THREESOME

A THREE-some is really a TWO-some
Our individual focus is always on the ONE we say does not matter
but does
Our THIRD, the odd ONE in
Our person of pleasure, convenience
We feast like having a turkey dinner, with all the fix' ins
It feels like a nice hot shower on a cold winter's eve
Going up, going down, going in, coming out
Succumbing to the pleasures and joy of togetherness of THREE,
meant for TWO
ONE to rest, ONE awake pondering
Morning argument inevitable
ONE had just a little too much fun, while ONE felt neglected
The decision for THREE in hopes of bringing TWO together
Ultimately realizing that ONE and ONE never equals THREE

POISON PASSION

Will you be the sultrier to steal thy heart
Shatter thy soul
Will you
Like the others leave me drowning in tear
Make off in the brilliance of sunshine instead of night
I pray for those who tasted my blood
Fell upon thy sword
The ones, unknowing of your hidden agenda
Mid-night rendezvous
Now are acquainted with death
Pray for their souls as we do our own hearts
Victims of your charm
Poisoned by your smile, beauty, and grace
The wicked passion of your presence

SNORT OF FANTASY

Love was expressed
I acknowledged, did not reciprocate
He could not understand why
Accused me of living the all too familiar lie
Implied love was not mine to have
Unless, Unless
I accepted my true feelings and acted on them accordingly
Our friendship of flirtation was at an end
His face burned red or was it blue
When he was informed that I had and was
Our friendship was based on respect and boundaries, no touching
or tasting
Understood that my lady was everything
Her eyes and scent caused my body to quiver in anticipation
That ours was the secret, a tease high on a shelf
A little box hidden from view, un-labeled
A snort of fantasy, the forbidden fruit
The sweet appetizer that will never be eaten
A precursor to the main course

Z

I warned you to check that monster before it ate you
Time after time it interrupted our most intimate moments
I fought that thing before
Dammit! I warned you, that beast would not stop
Not unless you killed it, or it killed you
Did I fail you, for not forcing you to fight!
When love found you, my heart sang a joyous song
It was true, a kind of love I couldn't provide, gentle hands, like your own
You ran away, out of my reach
You cannot outrun reality or the inevitable
I've wondered if she ever met the monster if she encouraged the fight
Did you allow her in, or fight her off
When I got the word that the monster was in control, and you beckoned me
I knew the fight was at an end, regrettably, I couldn't face that reality
The monster had devoured most of you, what remained, your heart
The very essence of who you were, in a matter of days that too would be eaten
Time has passed, and well, life continues
You have never left me, your presence is felt daily
It blankets me like warm sunshine
Comforts my heart
Seems you continue to provide me in ways I have failed you
My love is eternal, we'll meet again

15

STRENGTH

THE APPARATUS

The apparatus does exist
Though, not in the manner we're led to believe.
It's real, elusive dastardly
Prevents full potential
That thumb on our head
Foot on our coat tail
It's the negative thought that encourages doubt
That voice in our head questioning the very right of our existence
The road of righteousness hasn't been easy, how-ever, been long traveled
Un-daunted perseverance
Imagined giants there are, yes, but fooled we are not
Visible is the door behind which the machine hides
An apparatus and those who manipulate the mechanisms
Un-abashed conspiracies there in
Door of glass through which we see our reflection
Looking out on a world of un-imaginable promise

INSATIABLE INTOXICATION

Times of weakness
Wasted hours, days, weeks, months, years perched high atop my throne
A stool reserved as long as pockets were filled
Life planned through fantasy of heart
Psychological and philosophical lies
Masterfully convincing self of upward and forward mobility while still
Feeding on the false fruits of courage
Fed despair at great cost by fair weathered false friendship
Held hostage by cravings
Teased, taunted, and manipulated by souls inability to see beyond the glass
My prison of self-imposed shame
No longer intoxicated by insatiable urges
I stand tall unashamed, focused
Determined to walk life unwavering
A simple goal to keep feet planted
To follow a straight line without stagger

PERFECTION / REFLECTION

Flat head, large ears, toothless, naked, and vulnerable
All that you are, is who I am
Your perfection, is my reflection
My taught perception of who you are, should be, have become
A forced identity of selfish convenience
Couch caddy, door mat, punching bag
Pleasure tool who submits to my sexual whims
Comforting when the man within can't bear the pain or face the
reality of weakness
Hating the strength and fortitude of your conviction, allegiance,
mere presence
Yet, you remain
Tear filled glassy eyes that penetrate, starring, wondering why with
each episode
Evidence of your love or fear, felt deeply from your embrace when
comforting
Time after time after time
Always as I crumble on bent knee sobbing, begging for forgiveness
Again, and again and again
Time after time after time
Purple bruising on arms, neck and back
Ears that suffer the burden of misguided screams and verbal
assault
Yet, you remain
Silently, hiding in the shadow, waiting to comfort, enduring the
pain
Time after time after time Yet, you remain
My courage, my strength, my reflection

WE WAIT

We wait, bodies weakened, bedsores, intravenous drip
Our sunshine, a meal delivered by a smile, an empathizing touch
We wait for mask covered faces, the feel of latex gloves
We wait, longing for kind eyes, a gentle non-judge-mental voice
We wait for potential cures valued greater than life itself
We wait, forgotten
Our dreams of hope, crying out for
Empty souls
Broken hearts
Broken spirits
Broken minds
We wait for a future everlasting
We wait for the non-existent existence
We wait for the kind words of remembrance
We wait, for the waiting to end

STRENGTH & FRAGILITY

Backed against the wall
Hanging in wait, as mothers do
Nurturing instinct at the ready
A vacant womb still experiencing echoing pains
Calls of concern, non-existent
Calls of urgency, with over whelming frequency
The fragility of strength always over estimated
Tested time after time after time, always prevailing
Nerve racking, exhausting repetitious anticipation of woe
Bosom coupled in callused yet, gentle hands, baring offerings again
Breast milk rich in nourishment, like blood in veins, always flowing
Body of paper, strength of steel
Hair like Rapunzel, lowered from tender not yet fully healed scalp
Yet again, assisting in the ascend to sanctuary
Pleading voices of action, echoing in silence, fallen on deaf ears
Reminder that mother's cup, filled with righteousness is always
within reach
Always ready to quench the thirst and feed the soul of her hungry
child

TOM BOY

We used to call girls like you Tom Boy
That is, of course before, we knew, well, what you really were
It didn't come as a surprise, that my mother was one
My sister, the girl across the hall
Even a girlfriend, who became wife
All the indications were there
"I don't want to hold your hand"
"I don't need your help"
"What makes you think I can't take care of myself"
Strong independent women
Women who don't take no for an answer or an option
Women strong enough to use a smile and charm, when necessary,
without feeling diminished
Proud of the rug-rats born to them and abandoned by the likes of
me
Always, somehow, churning their cream into butter, turning life's
lemons into lemonade
Never afforded the option of giving up or giving in
Finding solace, tenderness, and comfort in the arms and between
the limbs of folk in kind who understand
Laying together weaving dreams of happiness with ease, trying to
avoid impending struggle because there will always be a struggle
Harriet's railroad
Sojourner's truth
Billie's fruit
Bessie's song of passion and strife
Strong determined women
Don't sleep on those stiletto heels
That skintight skirt
Those long legs in black silk stockings
That's the game, not the aim
These are strong women
Purposed women

Women who know the difference between a handout, a hand up, and a handshake

MOTHER'S WAR

I watched my mother navigate the kitchen as if it were a war ship, a destroyer.

For her it was entering battle, and nothing less.

Thanksgiving, her favorite holiday; it always brought out the best, sometimes even the worse. Everything had to be perfect, turkey, stuffed and basted, extra stuffing on the side and numerous other dishes prepped and ready to go.

We sat around silently like little soldiers awaiting her command. When the food was done, it was time to dine, hold hands and rejoice in his name, everything was complete.

We stuffed our faces, laughed, cried, and prayed for those who were long gone.

My mother smiled, leaned back with an all-knowing expression. Knowing there were plenty of leftovers and she did not have to reload to do battle for the next couple of days.

RIPPLING WAVE

Stones tossed across a pond
Calm waters broken with rippling wave
Life's steps
Repetitiously taken in frustration
Until success or the last stone tossed
Followed by a joyous chant "I did it."

MOTHER HERO

Every Hero doesn't wear a cape
Some stand their ground
Protect their young
Fight for what's right
Deliver on promises
Bare their souls
Nothing hidden
Tears flowing continuously
Pain, Joy
Always thankful for small accomplishments
Rejoicing in the fleeting moments of a job well done

POLITICS

I AMERICA

America is my home
This, is where I'm from
Generations past my ancestors
Were stolen from their homeland
Brought here in chains
Generations since
We have worked hard to be Americans
This, without choice
Because, for the most part, it's all we know
We have been given reluctant invitation of assimilation
Un-equal justice, after the fact
We are made to feel like occupying refugees
This state of reality was not asked for
It was forced upon us
We remain the only race of people in these United States
Not given the choice of coming to these shores of our own volition
There has never been an open armed welcome
Benefits or opportunity un-earned
Give us your weak, poor etc. never applied
Though we have managed advancement, assimilation
We as a people continue to struggle
Within the structure of a nation in denial
A nation of false promise, blinded by its own dark truths
A nation in fear of its own reflection
A nation unwilling to correct its misdeeds
Of challenging the truths of its origin
These are our American realities
"Not everything that is faced can be changed,
But nothing can be changed until it is faced."
James Baldwin

STILL ASLEEP

In my dream
There, in the distance, can you see it
A raccoon with a coyote in its mouth
A gazelle dragging the bones of a lion
A blue bird flying off, a hawk in its beak
Children are born to steward the earth
An equitable economy
A governing body that exists to serve
No meaning to the word REFUGEE
An end to hunger and homelessness
People no longer displaced by war
Unifying nations
Respect for religious freedoms
Love loyalty and commitment un-characterized or labeled
Worldwide coexistence, social cohesion
Open markets, fare trade
End to famine
Awakening from a peaceful sleep, without anxiety

WORDS WRITTEN ON PARCHMENT

Un-kept promises, the repetition of painful assault
Wounds that fail to mend, ignored, now festering
Cultural relativism and the road map to cohesion un-addressed
Our code of governance written on parchment, stained in blood
Documents of equality, allegiance, democracy, and the principles of social order
Words on parchment, re-interpreted for reasons of greed and supremacy
Words purposed and adopted in an era of enslavement by slave owners
Written in sunlight, overshadowed by lies of darkness, literally and figuratively
A plan for humanity in a time when inhumanity flourished
Words on parchment, tattered frayed with time, echoing the second stanza
"We hold these truths to be self-evident, that ALL MEN ARE CREATED EQUAL
That they are endowed by THEIR CREATOR WITH CERTAIN UNALIENABLE RIGHTS
Among these are life, liberty, and the pursuit of happiness......
Are these just ... words written on parchment for a selected few?

TAIL OF AN ORDINARY JOE

Hard to be an ordinary Joe, especially if you have a tail
People look with scorn
Some laugh, point, poke fun at the clothes you darn
Just to be yourself, live a simple life
Work hard, build a future without strife

Preconceived notions of what my tail represents
It's an appendage that keeps me balanced
Helps me to climb high as it's meant
It enables me to hold on with faith, against those of might
Those who lurk in the shadows insisting on fight

I walk a new terrain, unfamiliar territory
Tail wagging behind
Accepting and governed by a new set of rules
A land built on promise, of open arms and false pretense
Bound by invisible restraints, un-equal liberties at my expense

Fruit dangling from branches high above, once reached with ease
I am forced to tuck my tail and endure the tease
Climb only as high as my restraints allow
Quietly I sit, patiently, waiting for fruit to fall
Having learned,
I was never meant to reach the dangling carrot at all

TURNED AROUND

I turned my back, away from the absurdity of today's politics, not America
Ironically, I find myself still facing a wall
The wall, real or not has already manifested itself through the back channels of dark politics
America is larger than any individual, bigger, and stronger than any singular political party

My back is turned from politics that resist its founding ideals, closes its doors on the growing inevitability of change, choosing an un-just electoral college over the one person one vote promise.

America is suffering from fear, greed, the perpetuation of hate and the allowed flawed leadership that has closed its eyes on a nation and leaving **WE THE PEOPLE** without guidance or direction.

Our youth, the future of this nation, is scrambling, clutching at false hopes and distant promises.

The beauty of America has always been in the belief that all things are possible.

That the dreams and ideals of democracy will lead to prosperity.

We are all dreamers and must not allow dark politics to forget that a blind eye is exactly what it is, and that the road map defining our nation, drawn on parchment stands on its own, but, only when adhered to.

We are all dreamers

When we are allowed to dream, America stands tall, proud, strong, and un-matched

America is the land of infinite possibilities and opportunity, there is no greater nation than a nation that represents every culture and people on the entire planet.

It is time for the dark politics of America to turn around

THE CURE

A moment of normality
Is it so much to ask for a moment to simply breathe without stare or glare
This without fear of repercussion or judgment for wearing a mask
I am colorful, black, brown, white and rainbow
My love is universal, and the monster does not care
My mask is only, but one, weapon in the arsenal
Protection is a weapon against the consequence of non-action
I just want a moment of normality
To BREATHE and EXHALE
When will this end, or will it
The city is burning down around us
The pain and suffering continue without reprimand
Those committing crime by perpetuating lies, must be held accountable
These heinous acts of inhumanity should not go unpunished
The monster continues to devour all in its path without discrimination
Political parties be damned, we are all one nation
There will be no winning if we do not fight this thing together
This can only be done as human beings, not race, color, culture, or gender
The senseless death must STOP
The war must END
The only cure is US,
WE ARE THE CURE!

UNPREPARED

We have been here before
When the alarms rang out from Cherry Grove to The Castro
The stand was made, some say at Stone Wall. No one knows for sure.
We were unprepared then and we are unprepared now,
Despite having learned a terrible lesson.
Fingers were pointed, the dye cast.
We collectively prayed in tears, sat silent and shivered in fear.
Few at the top cared or dared to stand and be heard.
The onus was pinned on the afflicted
Heinous was the label for being human, true to self, proud and righteously so.
The echo of abstinence heard from ivory towers of shame
Ill-advised condemnation of the weak from a nation in peril
Eyes wide open were shut tight, until the smoke and fire of carnage invaded the halls of the
Misbegotten purist
The choking so severe, the pain so unbearable
The so-called righteous had no alternative than to open the windows of their hearts and souls.
They heard the screams only to realize that the burning stench of the afflicted was kin.
The rush to extinguish the fire far late
Yes, we have been here before and most likely will again
Still as in the past, we remain unprepared

SHATTERED GLASS

A brick, frustration
A plate glass window shattered
Sky filled with a million pieces of moon illuminated shard
The sound of fleeing feet through rain-soaked streets
Glass glistening in darkness reflecting the moons glow
Scattered diamonds of courage
Puddles dodged in flight
Message sent
Heart pounding a voice beckons in thunderous shout
Stop! Put your hands in the air

SENTIMENTAL

MAJESTIC MANIFESTATION

Out of darkness a rainbow appears
Beauty proceeded by thunder
The roar of a merciful God
Heavy rain, then calm
Clean smell of fresh air
Sunshine filtered through grey cotton silhouettes that journey our imaginations
Evaporating formations of wishful fantasies
Arched high above
No beginning, no end, no words
Majestic universal flag
Seamlessly unifying
Rewards abound
Twinkle of an eye, smile
Shared connectivity and joyful bridges
Hearts momentarily filled
Peaceful acknowledgements of fleeting promises
Our search for the pot of gold continues

HAPPINESS, TOUCH IT

Happiness
What is it, really
How does one measure it
Are there guidelines, criteria
You can feel it, but it cannot be touched, yet it touches you
Is happiness an emotional oxymoron
It is present when your heart smiles
The sight of someone dear
Observing the similarities of kinfolk
Being together as one of two
The connection and bond of family, despite the temporary rituals of love and hate
Mother's smile or tears at the embrace of a child
The pounding heart at the whisper yes to proposal
Eyes of the person that occupy your heart from across the room, in the anticipation of evening's conclusion
When heart for no apparent reason sings a contagious melody and your world smiles around you
Happiness, I can touch it

A DANCE LESS TRAVELED

Un-paved road
Rock and roll with each bump
Every ditch, toss, turn, thump
Bump and grind
Hugging at each bend
Hands in the air, blinding light
Radio broken, jerk side to side
Luminous signs to draw you closer
Bump, jump hold on tight
Juke joint in sight
Pause and sit one out for the night
Chicken roasted
Cornbread toasted
Pork ribs
Beef ribs
Fresh corn on the cob
That will do the job
A feast to behold
Music to my ears
The journey ends
Our dance begins

THE OLD STUMP

My family lived in the big house for generations
It was home
The only one I have ever known
Behind the house stood a massive oak tree
When my grandmother was a girl, she climbed that tree and swung
from its branches

There were many family gatherings under its leaves
Good times and those of sorrow
As time has passed and progress taken root
All that remain is an open space
A vacant lot and an enormous tree stump

Now that I am old and move kind of slow
It is nice to pass by plant myself on an old friend
Reminisce about good times long gone and the notion that this old
stump will always be home

PERFECT DAY

Haven't been to the river in a while
The peacefulness of the tribute benches
Seating is never a problem
Each dedicated to memories of loved ones passed

To Pearl, "We couldn't have had a more perfect day
Kory, "We will be together again to watch the ice melt at winter's
end, the docks being laid in summer and the long trains heading
north along the river"

Will someone record images of my memories
Mountains reflecting across calm waters
Vehicles circling its summit
Hovering clouds, baron trees

Frozen waterfalls in the distance
Sharp edged wings of seagulls cutting the wind
Skimming the waters in search of un-suspecting prey

Icy chills surround me
I sit in memory of the past enjoying the happiness that once
belonged to Pearl and Kory
Soon to be mine and those to follow

The whistle of long trains in winter
Sun bouncing off the sails of boats in summer
Memories forever
I could not have a more perfect day

I YEARN FOR A TIME LONG GONE

My heart yearns for a time long gone
A past that is still my present
A time when life was simple uncomplicated
When being efficient meant knowing your job and doing it well
A time when at the mention of apple, it was in relation to an apple
a day keeps the doctor away, you are the apple of my eye, and it
was heartfelt.
Cannot remember the last time I took a walk
Overheard someone say aloud
I love you
We have replaced intimate verbal communication with texting
Emotional response reduced to an emoji
A SMILEY FACE … REALLY
I have found myself using the word LOVE more frequently
Not frivolously
It is with meaning, feeling
The recipient needs to know it comes from the heart
I miss the actual pleasure and comfort of taking a walk
Strolling aimlessly
Surrounded by PEOPLE
Making CONTACT, brief encounters
A nod smile, glance of warm welcoming eyes without mask
Sitting, having real conversation
One that ends with a handshake, hug
If lucky the warmth of lips pressed gently against your cheek
A flirting whisper of affection
I yearn, I yearn……

MAGICAL MORNINGS AT THE GAZEBO

Sometimes I cannot wait to fall asleep
The coffee maker is set to brew
The alarm clock to ring just before dawn
Clothes neatly laid out
All there is left to do, close my eyes
The darkness of night will have its way
I awaken knowing that you are out there
Waiting, ready to embrace all
Selfishly I like to be first
Standing in your hollow
Feeling the warmth
Just you and I surrounded by mountains
We watch as the sun rise
Ice from up north floating down the Hudson
A brisk chill in the air
The magical singing of sparrows upon the wind
A dream fulfilled
Nature's gift
A simple morning view from the gazebo

WRITER

Typed on solid bond
Crushed and crumbled, hurled to its targeted bin
Missed in repetitious ritual
The tense yet passionate grip of pen, pencil
The harsh sound of fingers striking keyboard
Until words are aligned in heart and mind
Delivered from pain with pleasure and a sigh of accomplishment

UN-HEEDED WARNING

It has been some time since I have tended our needs
My neglect has brought us here
At the beginning, you fought hard, hoping I would change my mind,
I did not
I am aware now, that you were right, truly trying to be a friend
At the time, I was just a kid,
There did not seem to be any reason for concern, certainly not
alarm.
Truth be told, I resented your violent reminders from time to time
Grabbing my throat, bending me over until black spittle seeped
from the corners of my mouth
I could barely catch my breath
In retrospect, that was the point
Why is it, we never get IT, until it is too late, even though, there are
signs and warnings at every turn
In the end, always the same, when there is nothing to be done
We fill with regret, only if, could have, would have
That ever so resounding point of realization ringing in our mind
The bells of life notifying us death is about to rear its ugly head ...
but, you know
I am not afraid, made my peace for this selfish act

As I lay here staring at the ceiling awaiting the call, I just want to
thank you for trying
Wish I had heeded your warnings, no one deserves this fate

So, with much regret in passing, I remain affectionately yours

NATURE

A RIVER RUNS BELOW

The river rose above the bank
Happened sometime between twilight and dawn
It washed ashore aged driftwood, discarded plastics, and other
matter of scorn

Amongst the debris, minnows I think
Some still flapping, trying to hold on
Others exhausted, too weak to go on

Patiently waiting, like the homeowners above
For the wrath of nature to take its course

Eyes from river views, looking out in dismay at calm waters with
glistening reflection
Never looking down, avoiding detection
The carnage of nature, humanities footprint in the sand
Un-deniable evidence of man

Wave after wave
Tide upon tide
The river returns bearing gifts of excess and overindulgence
Small tokens, reminders of a debt long to be paid

NATURE'S SONG

The sound of nature a beautiful song
The lyrics, the strong will survive
The weak may fall prey

Human beings above all
given the gift of reason,
compassion, understanding
conscience to determine
who and what survives

Fear, poor judgment, not of nature
Just the natural flow of human beings
navigating a world of promise
Nature's song, sung out of tune

OVERCAST

Dark, overcast
Blaring horn, blinding beam
Hopeful the ride to a better life is on time
Patiently standing silent, staring into my personal abyss
Fog thick, air damp, morning nods
Steam rising, hovering above the river
Mountains reaching high above the clouds
A distant chant of geese and fowl
The lonely howl of coyote
The eyes of heaven open ever so slowly
Squishing sound of fallen leaves moist from dew
Travelers gather in quest of a way out or perhaps in
A chance of promise
A dream of prominence
Distant towers, horns of plenty
Discarded treasures of waste
Fortune overlooked, un-seen
Souls in need, ignored, un-acknowledged
A race to nowhere, always arriving on time
Our clocks punched
We begin counting down the minutes of our lives

REMINISCENT

Sun glistening brilliantly between fluttering leaves
Sparkling diamonds upon calm waters
A reflection of silhouettes
Geese flying high against a cloudless sky
Stirred from peaceful rest
I lay staring upward
My calm broken
Awakened by the familiar sound of honking horns
Sound reminiscent of busy metropolis
Eyes fixed high
The natural formation of victory
Singing in unison
Destination unknown
Determination a matter of awe
An arrow pointed
A target of serenity
Each component diligently towing the line
Following the leader
Un-breaking
Un-wavering
In their code of natural governance

LABOR OF LOVE

We grasp for life
Dangling, fluttering, clinging to the end
That cool crisp breeze
Our inevitable demise
Bodies withering
Drying skins of fascination
Discoloring of change
Sun bleached veins
Cruel harsh un-forgiving wind
Mother's annual metamorphosis
Ripped from her who bared and lost the fruit of life
Nutrients that nourished the souls of many
Her labor of love
Gone to begin anew
Hearts and souls of the un-knowing
Pleasured by her annual gift
Freely we let go
Falling silently
Floating to the ground
Our lives slip away
Brown, yellow, orange, red, often green, un-ready and un-fulfilled

OVERDUE ACCOUNT

Brisk chill, cool breeze
Blue skies and golden sun
Cloud formations in the distance
Sudden cold harsh un-forgiving wind
Chimneys alive with the smell of burning cedar
Wood oven baked bread and apple pie
Brilliant rays of sunlight beaming through trees
Patterns of leaves blanket the road
Dry brittle crunch beneath my feet
Wildlife scatter with each step
The fruit of nature at terms with an un-timely fate
Frozen waterfall, non-flowing brook
Fish that spawn trapped in icy graves
Migratory birds' stead fast
Tricked by our misdeeds
Blame be the mother of us all
A most un-willing accomplice
A price for-seen, but, un-imagined
Our feast at its end, payment long overdue
Patiently time abide
Nowhere to run or hide
Time to pay the tab

HAPPY UNDER THE BRIDGE

Trolls are happy under the bridge
I brought one home, under the impression I was saving its life
It appeared discarded, un-wanted, but that's how trolls are
Never occurred it was content
Rolling in the mud and filth
Shielded from the sun and curious eyes, anonymous
The dampness, humidity lingering like fog, was a good thing

Now, it sits curled in a corner
I must get it back, undo what has been done
Misting does not seem to make a difference
Removed from what I now know, was its natural environment
My heart and soul tell me it wants to go home
Un-fortunately it cannot in present condition

Sometimes leaving nature to take its course, un-interrupted is a
good thing
Its round sad eyes just stares, does not know anger or hate, just
fear, acceptance, adaptation, and an overwhelming desire to
survive.

HUMAN INTEREST

HIEROGLYPHS

Words, images like water that once flowed through canyons
Still, but telling
Shared fragments of souls, lives lived
Markers of existence
Evidence that we were
We meant
We mattered
Ancient tales of encouragement
Distant notes of laughter
Whispers of yearnings for love
Visceral out pour of pain, loss, despair
Harmony with nature, dismissed
Directions for continuance, ignored
Selfless cohesion, non-existent
The symphony of our lives, music played in silence
Pieces left behind markers of who we were
Our legacy imprinted on the earth
A tale of reckless stewardship, eventually deciphered
Hieroglyphs of our times

A GIFT OF CONTINUANCE

People and trees live threatened
Large numbers inhabiting densely populated land masses
Each population rising vertically, tall firm, resilient
Resistant to the cold harsh reality of the inevitable winds of change
Deep rooted seeds of distant lands
Once tossed to the skies, blown in every direction
Nature's gift of unity and cohesion
An amassing of lives without boundary, race, color, gender, or
religion
Now at odds, the battle of survival impending
The stakes, high, a planet in peril
A war against ourselves, no winners, or losers
Just a chance of harmony and, continuance of existence

THE RABBIT DIED I CRIED

I cried when the rabbit died
Its death was both blessing and equally a time of fear
Fatherhood and support, was instilled in me at an early age
There was no fear of that
I fortunately had great examples, a stepfather, shoeshine man at
the subway entrance
Even the homeless gentleman on the corner
The fear in my heart and pain in my gut, centered around, my
inability to protect my child
Pure innocence, born into a world of hostility and violence,
A world with no regard for life in shades of black and brown
I feared for the challenges and obstacles my child would have to
over come
I feared my capabilities in providing the necessary skill set for
survival, would not be adequate
I feared for this world's civil normality and peaceful continuance
I feared the rabbits born for people like me will disappear and we
will be no more
I feared the loss, as my child wonders off into this world of false
promise

WHAT NEEDS TO BE SAID

We talk, speak out
How often do we, really mean what we say … say what we mean
Sincerely, care about our words, their meaning
The damage, hurt or good the effect has on the recipient
Is it meaningless verbiage thrown into a vast pit of emptiness
Noise of convenience, we avoid saying what's is really on our mind
When someone is being un-truthful, and we know it
Instead of calling them out
We keep silent waiting for the next verbal assault
Well, never again, I intend to say what needs to be said
I think about those once laughable relationship assaults
The hurtful un-necessary outburst from those we hold dear
Their misdirected anger, spewed in our faces
Why, because we allow it
Somehow there is this misconception that it is ok to hurt us
The assumption being, we know they don't mean it
After an apology, treat of sort
They're most assured forgiveness
While on the other hand, and there always is the other hand
Feelings of those hurtful words that linger, festering in our hearts
Wounds that never seem to heal,
by chance they do, scar tissue doesn't go away
It's always there, a lasting reminder of pain past, or in some
instances
Continued … continued and continued, until we speak up
Increase our self-worth, simply by saying … what needs to be said

EVERYDAY ADVENTURE

Waking up to clear skies
The sound of chirping birds, honking horns
The smell of fresh brewed coffee
The warm eyes and pure heart of the person I call partner
That gaze, the one that takes my breath away
A faint and reassuring smile of what the day promises
Iron rails
Shoulder to shoulder with strangers
The gleam in their eyes
Warm smiles and mutual morning nods
Acknowledgement that we are all in this together
Singular souls entering one another's lives
Touching hearts for only a moment without expectation
Life is good

JUST NOISE

Wish I was a better human being
A person willing to answer the call without fear or delay
Not having to weigh the feeling of negative throwback...
questioning what's on a person's mind, am I putting myself in
danger simply for doing what I was taught is the right thing
Encountering the call is a daily occurrence
The homeless person asking for hand outs
Artists performing their craft on the streets for change because
there are no jobs
A couple sitting on the sidewalk with child begging as a last resort...
It is not difficult to hear the call
It yells so loud and frequently that we answer it abruptly and
spontaneously just to make it stop
simply for a moment of silence...
Without even knowing what the noise is about
I've placed my hands over my ears,
shutting my eyes so tight tears escape
Just to block the noise, it doesn't go away...
It gets louder and louder until I start screaming and become the
noise begging for help and assistance to make it stop
Eyes just stare and journey on
Avoiding any contact or humanitarian connection
Ignoring heartfelt tears, of stories shared in kind of taking that right
turn when the right turn was left
Gambling on a better life
On the hope of a two-month point spread, losing to the curb
Realizing in the much too late descent ... we are all the same
Some of us singing, some crying, others yelling
In the final analysis, it's all just noise

BEACON OF LIGHT

"Try and be home before dark" Mama used to say "I'll leave the
light on for you"
The original saying was, I'll leave a candle burning
'Never knew what that really meant
Passengers fleeing enslavement aboard Harriet Tubman's
Underground Railroad did
Every stop, a window, a lit candle, or oil lamp indicating a safe
haven
Homes of conductors putting themselves and family in harm's way
for the greater good
The humanitarians, stewards of life and freedom shining in
darkness
A light to guide the way
A light of sanctuary
A beacon of hope signaling from afar that freedom is within reach
As the years have passed that beacon of light, candle in the
window have come to represent many things
The gleam in the eyes of a child who finally understands a lesson
taught
Reaching soil of a foreign land to escape persecution, in hopes of a
better life
Hope in the vision of moving beyond the past and fulfilling the
dream
Believing in the power and promise of a man standing on a
mountain yelling
"Yes, we can, yes we can, YES WE CAN"
A light in his eyes, fire in his heart
Raising torches at the entrance of nations
Opening borders, guiding the way ...
Following a star, a beacon of light, a candle in the distance, a
promise of hope...
No matter the color of house or forces that rule
The winds of tyranny and storms of evil will never douse the light or
blow out the flame

The faces have changed, but the language of tyranny is the same
Evil dwelling in darkness, afraid of the approaching sands and the
evitable Changing face of a nation

STORIES TOLD IN SILENCE

A thousand tongues planted in the ground
Each reaching up silently from beyond
Waving in the air, flapping voiceless
The stories of old told anew
They mimic a soundless chant
Fresh be the version without pain, without suffering
Crying replaced by song and joyous shout
Pitched to only what the eyes can see
What the heart can bear
Screams of visceral out pour
Tongues on spikes, reaching out
Hands eager to touch, to be held, saved
Waving in the wind like fresh grown grass
Awakened by sunlight or thunderous storm
Nurtured for their righteousness
Honored for their earthly sacrifice

CHANGE IS COMING

I have looked to the heavens for guidance
Life has become frightening, almost unbearable
For better or worse, it's hard to tell
The past is ever so present
An un-yielding cycle of hatred has manifested, near and far
Our planet appears to rotate in the opposite direction
Nature is un-a-lined
History is repeating itself
Ivory towers are in denial
People are rising up
The strain of merely existing has become over whelming
The nation is in service of an un-serving constitution
There's a dark cloud of fear, a blanket of suspicion
The nation is drowning in its own tears
Blind eyes are wide open
We're choking, please help
We can't breathe, we can't breathe
Must we bear the burden for those who follow, as did those to
guarantee our survival
Un-selfishly make the sacrifices of continuance
This, for those who choose not to believe or understand
We have to stand-up, be counted, for the young and those who
can't, there is no failure in doing so
Just the regret of doing nothing

HIGH STAKES GAMBLE

Out of my Madison Avenue gig at around ten-ten
Trying to make my ten-twenty bus
It's always a rush, rush situation
So, I move it move it
I'm making my way, dodging cars, jumping on and off the sidewalk
Three blocks six minutes to go
I notice this shadow, all up in my ass
Guess they noticed me too, because he or she ran on pass, up
ahead three car lengths
The shadow dressed in black, head to toe
Street dark, no one around
I'm no punk, but a baseball bat would have served me well
Kept thinking, am I being set up, or am I being paranoid and
judgmental
Better safe than sorry
I pray it's not someone about to challenge me to stand my ground,
their ground, our ground
Trying to make a point that only woke folk understand
It's a dangerous gamble where the stakes are high
Foolish choices can result in great loss
I'm just saying

MUD SCROLLS

Scrolls rolled in mud, planted to ground
Silent invisible voices, stories of old told anew
A silent chant of binding all life, in one world, with one goal
A version without pain, without suffering
Crying replaced by song and joyous shout
Pitched only to what the mind's eye can see
What the heart can bear
Screams of visceral out pour
Ancestral tongues rolled in scroll
An un-deciphered language reaching out
Invisible hands eager to touch, to be held, saved
Dust of mud curled like fresh grown grass
Preserved by sunlight and thunderous storm
The words of righteousness
Sealed within time honored earthly sacrifice
The history of humankind, layered in the banks of our shores
Embedded in the walls of canyons
Invisible layers of our existence
Voices shouting out, crying out and singing out, in joyful silence

THE SKIN THAT I'M IN

The skin that I'm in is not who I am
It's what people perceive me to be, at face value.
Sure, it gives insight, like where I'm possibly from or perhaps, what
atrocities my people might have endured or what ignorant people
have told you to generally expect from someone of my culture.
Doesn't matter what I'm wearing or how I carry myself.
Ninety Percent of the time the reaction is the same, shock, fear,
uncertainty.

Some time ago, I had an encounter with a young man on the A train
in New York City.
He was in my words and at first glance panhandling. (See how this
works, conditioning, get the picture)
He was dressed decently, pants up, shirt tucked, there was no
smile.

Along with his routine, I've taken to referring to all these train
panhandling encounters as routines.

Seems you cannot take a ride in this city without encountering a
hard luck story or the intimidating dude that announces he is not
out busting heads and robbing.
Instead, he's asking for handouts like everyone should be grateful
therefore more generous.

Anyway, this young man while soliciting what he called donations
asked if anyone had a prospective job lead.
Well, besides me, a few others looked up. When he got to me, I
shook his hand placing a folded dollar bill in his palm.

"Don't lose focus or hope brother, things change, it gets better I've
been there, just a matter of time."
I will never forget his all-knowing smile.

He bent down so we were eye to eye and calmly said. "Brother, the people out here, they don't see me as a person, a man. All they see is this shell from THEIR hell. Before I open my mouth, you can see it in their eyes. False notions, preconceived biases, decisions concerning life, MINE! Dismissed with the shrug of a shoulder, really doesn't matter. Tomorrow is another day; as for this skin that I'm in, well, I will be wearing it again."

With that he leaned up, took my hand, and gave me a wildly over exaggerated handshake. "You Take Care, or any way you can get it, Feel Me?"

The doors of the train opened, he stepped out and in an instant, he was gone and in the palm of my hand a folded dollar bill.

PRIMA FACIE

Short Fiction

Prima facie, at first impression before proof or investigation based on what appears to be truth, conjecture.

A perception or opinion based on a notion of so-called societal norms.

SHORT FICTION

PUBLISHING ACKNOWLEDGMENTS

Dark Perspectives
Published 2018: Writing for Peace, Dove Tales, "Empathy in Art - Embracing the Other"
Sacrifice Paid Forward
Published 2019: Writing for Peace, Dove Tales, "One World - One People"
Fractured Soul
Published 2016: Writing for Peace, Dove Tales
"Family & Cultural Identity"

SACRIFICE PAID FORWARD

(Story One)

Chapter one: Befitting End

There was a pounding on the front door. Annoyed I lifted myself from the sofa and cautiously tip-toed to see who was there. I could see Ole Casey through the peek hole leaning against the door frame. As I slowly pulled the door open Casey stumbled in collapsing halfway across the threshold. He lay there retching in pain clutching his stomach, trying to hold in what was left of his gut. His eyes were bulging in fear.

Miss. Martha McCrea his wife, was standing across the hall leaning against her apartment door. Her head bowed and bobbing like the big-headed dolls, replicas of baseball players, and such. Just hanging there, her arms were at her side. One draped around the shoulders of her nine-year-old daughter Jolie whose fragile little body was wrapped around her thigh. Her spirit broken, hiding in the safety of her mother's shadow. Tears streamed down her cheeks, a trickle of blood down her little leg. Martha's second arm flexing at her side, a rusted butcher's slaughter knife clutched in her hand, blood dripping to the floor.

Theirs was a story destine to end tragically. An appropriate conclusion befitting the beast. Miss. Martha's eyes glazed over with tears, shivered, and stuttered as she spoke. "You gonna save him Doc. Edward?" At the time I was on one knee, my hand on Casey's neck trying to feel his pulse. There were gurgling sounds from blood backing up in his throat, he was drowning. Having heard the cries from abuse and the pain of drunken rage I was acutely aware of what needed to be done. I dragged Casey across my threshold and told Miss Martha to get rid of the knife, she had forgotten it was still flinging about in her hand. She repeated, with tears rolling down her cheek and dripping from her chin. Insistently she demanded to know "You gonna save him Doc?" I knew that if I answered yes, she'd finish the job.

The body language was transparent. I could sense the fear in her heart at what might transpire if Casey survived. Taking a deep breath I said "Don't worry yourself about that Miss Martha. Some things are best left to God. Now go on, go inside, tend to Jolie. Wash everything down and get rid of that knife." Our eyes met in silent acknowledgement as to what was about to happen, she nodded and slowly backed into her apartment pulling Jolie at her side. When I was certain they were safe, I too re-entered my room and closed the door. Casey un-able to move or speak just lay there on the linoleum floor gurgling and bleeding out.

I wrestled with my options and the possible consequences, most of all my integrity in regard to the Hippocratic Oath I'd sworn. In the real world I toiled to understand what the oath really meant. To protect and preserve human life, I weighed the pros and cons of Casey's life, as I knew it. Not playing God, just being a man with all the teachings and personal learned experiences of life. I existed in a world where the fractured are cast aside, un-seen except by one another. An urban sub-culture, an under-belly world that teeters on the brink of civilization. An outcast society surviving and maintaining itself by adhering to its own laws. Rules governed by animal instinct, God fearing reality and common sense. I walked to the cabinet above the sink, that's where I stored the bottle of courage. There were only two glasses in the entire apartment, both in the sink dirty. The gurgling continued; blood bubbles appeared in the corners of Casey's mouth. I ran water and rinsed one glass, no need for two. The last time Casey had a drink that was it. Bottle in hand I pulled a chair from the table and sat down. Two fingers were poured and thrown back, and repeated. I'd made my decision. It took Casey an hour and fourteen minutes to succumb. My flat was one room with a small kitchen in the corner. It was located on the second level of a three story walk up. Everyone on the floor shared one bathroom with a shower. At the end of the hall, hanging on the wall was an old pay telephone. It was so close to the window that we used the windowsill as a seat. During early morning hours just before daybreak it was the most comforting spot in the world. You could sit there with your legs dangling on the fire escape. Quietly, at peace watching as the sun rose. Pigeons landed on the railings, bright orange and red bursts of heaven birthing a new day washing away the stench of yesterday.

We called the building the Bridge because it was like a resting place between nowhere and the end. Most folks like myself, moved in at the lowest point after losing everything. That point in life when the bottom seems as high as the top, or perhaps just being poor. Thankful for just having a place to rest exhale, regain composure hoping to someday bounce back. Very few in my time have ever left the Bridge, on two feet; that is. The Bridge is a line between the end and a new beginning. Certainly, the longest extension in life I've ever tried crossing. You can look out as far in the distance as you like you'll never glimpse the other side. 'Just gotta keep your head up and never stop walking forward. I threw back another finger or two and checked Casey's pulse once again, didn't need him coming to in the middle of an investigation. I opened my door and leaned over the railing, shouting down to Charlott. She was the owner of the building and resided on the first floor, "Miss. Charlott you up?" I yelled repeatedly. Miss. Martha's door was ajar. She looked at me in question. I could tell she hadn't slept. Who could? I put my finger to my lips and motioned for her to remain silent and go back inside she complied. Charlott opened her door and yelled upstairs. "Doc, what the hell is wrong with you, its three fuckin' AM?!" "I know"

I replied, "Look, Casey got himself in a bit of trouble. I need you to call an ambulance and the cops" "Cops, why can't you do it?" She yelled. "I don't have any money, not even one thin dime. You have a house phone, come on Miss. Charlott, I think he's dying." "Well save him, you're a doctor! Aren't you?" Those words, like shards of glass in my brain, bouncing around like pennies in a child's bank "Shit woman! Just call, will ya?" She slammed her door in a huff, ten minutes later the police arrived.

"Upstairs" I heard Charlott say. By this time my door was wide open, Miss. Martha's door ajar, she was peeking out.

"Where's the injured person?" The detective asked, I pointed to my apartment; "There."

"What happened?" he asked.

"I don't know, he banged on my door. When I opened up, he fell down. I dragged him in and did what I could. Then we called for an ambulance."

"Do you know him?" The detective asked.

"Sure" I replied, "He lives across the hall. I didn't knock on his door" "Why not?" the detective demanded.

"Well, because he has a little girl and a wife." I turned from Miss. Martha's view and drew the officer closer.

"His wife is a little slow, she doesn't properly understand things. Know what I mean?"

"So, explain to me, why he would knock on your door instead of his own?"

"Probably because he knows I was a doctor; once." The detective notices the bottle and glass on the table.

"Looks like that was the second wrong choice he made tonight."
"What do you mean? I did everything I could do, there was just nothing more to be done, nothing I could do!"

"Yeah well, that's obvious." He replied with a smirk.

The police took a number of pictures and questioned a few residents. Even though they noticed Martha peeking through the partially opened door, Jolie wrapped around her side. They never spoke a word to her. Perhaps because I mentioned she was slow, which of course wasn't the truth. Maybe it could have been the overall appearance of circumstance. Martha was a woman of average stature, between forty-six and fifty years. She kind of just dragged about. Always seemed worn, tired, and over worked, an appearance dominated by a sloth like demeanor. Her clothes were old and tattered; she walked around on the backs of flat shoes that offered no support, just separation from the cold hard wood plank floors.

When the authorities were finished, their investigation completed. They packed their equipment and begin the process of removal. Last to go was Casey's corpse. It had been placed inside of a black rubber body bag. Having been a medical professional I knew this was to be expected, yet somehow I anticipated seeing a stretcher being carried out covered with a white sheet. Martha seeing Casey being taken away, softly pounded her fist against the door frame. Tears flowing down her cheeks and again, dripping from her chin, nose running and sniffling. She lifted the front of her tattered dress and wiped her eyes with the hem. Jolie hugged her mother tighter and began to weep.

Taking notice, in a sign of humanity rarely exhibited in this community, the lead detective in an act of empathy approached

Martha for the first time and touched her shoulder. Jolie looked on watching from behind, a rag doll with yellow yarn hair hanging at her side. The detective offered his condolences. "We'll see that he's taken care of Ma'am, don't you worry it'll be fine." Martha nodded in acknowledgement as the officials departed. She raised her head for the second time that night. Once again, our eyes met, she mouthed the words "Thank you Jesus." The corners of her mouth curled in what could only be interpreted as a smile. I nodded, pleased somehow that a burden had been lifted, but wondered at what cost. I turned to enter my room and caught a glimpse of little Jolie; in her wide-eyed innocence, she stared up at her mother's rarely seen smile. As my door closed Martha continued the praise of long sought-after answered prayers.

Everyone who lived at the Bridge knew who Casey was, not to mention the dirty tricks of life and lowest deeds of humanity he'd performed to survive. He'd stood about five feet six inches tall with a basketball type belly mass. He dressed in the latest neighborhood thug fashion, bright colored loud clothing that most people found unacceptable. However, in the neighborhood they were considered a symbol of status, mostly because of the high cost of purchase. That's how it's always been; you didn't have to have much, but, if you had more than your neighbor. In the eyes of those who couldn't afford it, you were looked up to. In some cases considered special.

Many people disliked Casey. Had it not been for his association with the men who owned the corner bodega and ran the local numbers racket, many a man would have taken him out years ago. That is, if not for fear of retribution. It was the only thing that kept him safe. Casey made a lot of money for those guys on the corner and as long as the money flowed, they had his back. Now that he was gone, there were definitely questions that needed answering.

Jackson "Crush" Ruiz was the ringleader of the Bodega crew. He was tall, young, and very handsome; some even thought he was pretty. His hair was slicked back, pearl white teeth and manicured nails. It all made him a standout; the women loved it. Rumor had it he got his moniker Crush because so many neighborhood ladies liked him. Truth be told, it came years earlier after taking a sledgehammer and bashing in the skull of a former bully and rival who had disrespected him in public. He needed to make a statement and did. From that point he was neighborhood royalty and that was only out of fear. It didn't take long for Jackson "Crush" Ruiz to come knocking. In fact, it was only a few days later. Charlott was standing out front, showing off her new white laced blouse. She usually held the post questioning everyone's comings and goings. When Ruiz and his crew approached she stood defiant, didn't move, or utter a word. As they entered the building and passed, she promptly entered her apartment. Her place was the only two-bedroom unit in the entire building. It also had a separate bathroom. The men walked halfway up the step and stopped. Ruiz shouted, "Doc Ed," I didn't answer. No use in trying to be brave. I thought they'd come for me. I was scared, I pulled the door open and made like everything was normal. It was anything but. "Who's that calling my name?" There were two of them in the building and one out front. "Well I'll be damned" Ruiz said laughing, "There is a doctor in the house."

He had a big mischievous grin. His pearl white teeth gleaming like diamonds. "What do you want?" I asked. "You really don't want to play stupid Doc; You know why I'm here. I want to know what happened to my boy" "I don't really know, seems he got into it with somebody who got the best of him. Then he comes knocking on my door. I tried but there was nothing I could do." "Well Doc, did he say anything, like who did it?" "No, not a word, he could barely talk. He was holding his guts in with both hands. Nobody could talk in that condition." "God damned!" Ruiz yelled and pounded the banister. His henchman said, "Boss I need the toilet" Ruiz turned angrily and snapped "Well go, do you need me to hold your fuckin' hand!" I pointed to the bathroom. "You sure he didn't say anything?" "No, nothing" I replied. "What about his ole lady, you think she knows something?" At that point I knew I needed to come up with an excuse. Why not stick to the original. His next move was to bang on her door. The henchman came out the bathroom. Ruiz looked him up and down. "I thought you needed to crap?" Walking down the steps the man turned "I just as soon shit in the hall." I'll be out front" Ruiz shook his head and turned his attention back to me. "Well, what about her?" "She's slow" I said "Dumber than a sack of doorknobs, and they got a nine-year-old girl that rivals her mother in intelligence. Sometimes you can't tell the mom from the kid. You'll get nothing there. No woman with half a mind would have put up with that piece of trash. You knew him." Ruiz just listened as I spoke out of turn. I realized my mistake a little too late "Look, I'm just saying, after he died, well you can imagine what people say and none of its good. Most of it is about that little girl. Casey had devil problems. That's all I got to say on the matter, don't know what happened to your boy." "Well sooner or later, the truth will rise, and someone will fall, we'll talk again Doc." With that he turned and walked down the steps.

Charlott had come back out into the vestibule. She looked at Ruiz and rolled her eyes. He didn't take kindly to that and stopped. He asked, "That night of the killing, you hear anything Miss?" Defiantly Charlott said, "I got nothing to say to you or your thugs." He smiled and grabbed a hand full of her just treated afro hair. He yanked her head backward forcing her against the wall. His knee in the base of her spine. "I asked you a question." Noticing the commotion the two members of his crew came running in. They stood in the doorway. I kept quiet and crouched down peeking through the banister. "I'm Sorry" cried Charlott "I'm sorry" she pleaded. "I didn't see or hear anything, I swear, please…" Ruiz let her go, wiping his hand and the oil of her hair on her new white blouse.

"Good" he said then shouted, "We'll be talking again real soon Doc, count on it!" As Crush Ruiz exited the building Charlott yelled out knowing that Crush was no longer within ear shot. "MOTHER FUCKER, YOU MOTHER FUCKER!" She entered her apartment and slammed the door.

I stood and turned, there in the corridor standing halfway out of his room was Chung. He was an aging immigrant American of Asian descent, Chung moved into the Bridge three years earlier after being discharged from a hospice. He was diagnosed with a terminal inoperable illness and thought to have had only months remaining. Fortunately or not, Chung survived, not to mention out living his medical insurance. Having given away and donating all his worldly possessions, he was discharged and virtually penniless. Nowhere to turn he arrived at the Bridge. Again in unfortunate circumstance, not like the rest of us. The possibility of Chung bouncing back wasn't an option, this was it. When he left there is no doubt, it was going to be in a body bag. "I hear everything, Doc Edward, they no good scum of earth. Miss Charlott no call cops, I call cops, I not afraid." "No Chung, it's alright, we don't need any more trouble, they're gone, let it be, just let it be." "If you say so Doc Edward, you good man, I see what you do for lady and girl, apartment there." He pointed toward Martha's door. "No Chung, I didn't do anything, hear me?" I was about to panic. "You save her life, protect girl. He scum too, glad he gone. You do good Doc Edward." "Ok Chung, thank you. No cops, our secret ok?" "Ok, you say so Doc" "I do Chung, I do …thank you" Chung nodded his head and entered his room. Taking a deep breath and sighing, I followed suit.

Chapter Two: Brick House

Tensions continued to run high in the months following Crush Ruiz's visit to the Bridge. Even though there wasn't any solid evidence or proof of what transpired, Crush had his suspicions. His goons would occasionally come by and harass the tenants. Everyone treaded lightly and kept their guard up. The Bridge experienced a study flow of transients. Many who weren't in it for the long haul, just a pit stop moving forward, that said, in my experience once in, you never know how the dice will play, one bad roll can make all the difference.

Out of all, the most unlikely tenant stayed, the distinguished Dr. Ronald Clark. He was an unusual gentleman, well dressed and versed. He was in his late forties and carried himself with such distinction. He always wore the same outfit and colors, plaid jacket, white shirt, black tie and black shoes, pants, always black. As time passed and it was evident that he wasn't leaving, the gossip started. Mr. Ron as I began calling him, appeared very much out of place, rumor had it he taught school at one of those Ivy League colleges, which I assumed would make him a Ph. D, doctor, or something close. He didn't appear to be a drinker or druggie, just lost, like the rest of us. According to the gospel of Miss Charlott, he was hiding out from the law. That being the case, she also let it be known that if anyone disturbed the Doc, they would be out on their butt. One really couldn't blame her or argue the point, seeing that he paid six months' rent in advance; especially since most of us were at least two months behind.

Eventually our paths did cross, and I started referring to him as Dr. Ron. He lived in the room right above mine. The tenants on the third floor praised him. They said twice a week he'd get in the bathroom with a whole box of cleaning supplies and scrubbed until the place smelled as sanitary as a hospital. Myself, I just cleaned mostly when I needed to use the facilities. Miss Charlott never paid anyone a decent dime to clean. Considering the load of crap, no pun intended, they had to deal with, most just abandoned the project halfway through without notice, simply walked off the job. So it was always left up to the tenants, God knows Charlott wasn't about to get her hands dirty.

Prior to having met Dr. Ron formerly, I saw him talking to Mrs. Martha in the stairwell. They departed the building around the same time in the morning. Martha had to drop little Jolie off at school, the Doc just went off on his way. He appeared kind and respectful. I'd not seen Martha interact with anyone, that is, with a smile since Casey's demise. It appeared she re-joined the living, a far cry from the life she led prior. Little Jolie is the only thing that kept her from going over the edge. She got a part time job stocking shelves at the large market about a half mile away. It really did her good, gave her a sense of confidence and strength, and it showed. Dr. Ron took a shining to her, seeing that did my heart a world of good.

As time passed Chung's health started to deteriorate. Every day he'd set out on a walk, never making it any further than the front door and stoop. That's where he'd plant himself and chit- chat with Miss Charlott. That I must say was a strange combination. The woman thumbed her nose at everyone but took a genuine comfort in baring her soul and not to mention gossip to Chung who barely spoke or understood English. Martha developed a knack or you could say a penchant for baking. On the weekends she and little Jolie baked enough goods for the whole building. The smell alone was euphoric, the pastries and cakes she came up with, none of us could afford, well maybe except the Doc. We'd spend fifty cents on a devil dog or ring-ding and called it a luxury. I asked her why she hadn't thought about selling some of her goods to help make ends meet. Turns out she had but didn't sit well with the notion because she got all the ingredients for free. Busted bags of flour and sorts that couldn't be sold were given to employees who wanted it. Baking was a blessing; it gave her an activity she and Jolie could do together. I'm certain there was more to it. Subconsciously I imagine it was also a way of paying it forward. After Casey, she strutted around with Jolie, proudly displaying heartfelt blessings she wore proudly on her shoulders.

In all of it, I wondered how I'd personally be viewed by God, for my part, can't say I wasn't troubled. There were many and continued sleepless nights. In the over-all, I can't say I wouldn't repeat my actions. She and the situation restored a piece of me I thought was long gone, reconciling hard choices, doing the heart's bidding. Taking charge and understanding the nature of humanity and the raw wealth of sacrifice. Happiness just for the sake of being alive, appreciating what you have without wish or envy. The seasons changed rapidly, it seemed we raced through summer and barely had a chance to witness the harvest colors of autumn. The early frost and brisk winter's chill sent everyone into hibernation and seclusion. I got out as often as possible and walked in the blistering wind, leaves stirred and blowing like mini tornados half colored and browning, many frosted, holding and dangling awaiting their evitable demise.

The cold of winter arriving early was upon us. Chung, who never deviated from his daily pilgrimage to the stoop no matter what the weather, always accompanied by Miss Charlott who found it in heart to provide him with a much needed and appreciated cup of tea from time to time. Often she wrapped a blanket around his shoulders. Every morning like clockwork Dr. Ron, Mrs. Martha and little Jolie would go running out in the early morning hours. We finally had a sense of normalcy and civility it felt good. I got up every morning and sat on the hall window seat next to the telephone. There was something about having coffee and watching the city come alive.

There was a steady stream of delivery and garbage trucks throughout the boroughs, all weaving in and out of traffic, always trying to stay ahead of one another. It was like a competition, whipping around corners pausing only at the pedestrian crosswalk, only if they had to. Most people just navigated the gauntlet and continued on their merry way, dangers notwithstanding. As I sat sipping coffee all departing tenants waved and extended morning greetings. Despite the financial hardships and emotional circumstance the small blessings were quite apparent. Neither of us had any more than the other and knew it. That bit of knowledge united us. We were all in this together.

Right before the Christmas holiday bright lights tinsel and the smell of roasted chestnuts Dr. Ron appeared to have taken up with what we used to refer to as a Brick House. She was tall and very curvy. She only made appearances late at night, coming in and going out. I'd overheard Dr. Ron's conversations from upstairs, barely audible but you could definitely make out a woman's voice. There was also the constant annoying sound of high heels prancing about the place. "Girl you look stunning, can't wait for you to spread those cheeks." Sayings like that were always followed by bursts of laughter. Not too long after I'd hear her leaving for the night. The heels made a distinctive sound. Not being nosey, just curious, I'd crack my door just in time to see her legs and behind through the banister as she went down the steps. I can't be certain, but I believe she was aware I watched from time to time. One evening she paused at the perfect spot, hoisted her skirt up high, way too high and adjusted her stockings. I let out a huge gulp she chuckle pulled down her skirt and journeyed on, giggling all the way out the door. This activity continued on for a while, the comings, and goings. Eventually it got the unwanted attention of Miss Charlott. She suspected something was askew. Had it not been for the fact that she thought an additional person was staying in Dr. Ron's room and there weren't any extra coins coming her way it wouldn't have mattered.

Two days before Christmas late one evening Charlott was hanging colorful lights and a wreath in the hallway just beyond the vestibule. In walks Brick House, she pauses to remove her shoes so as not to make any noise and looks up before entering and lays her heavy lashed and mascara eyes on Charlott. Dumb founded and unable to get out a word, Charlott just stares. Brick House does a complete about face. I mean whipped around, heels in hand and beat it up the street bare feet and all, disappearing into the night. That was the last we saw of the Brick House until New Year's Eve.

It was tradition at the bridge for everyone to come into the corridors just before midnight with whatever beverage they had or could afford. We were laughing and talking up a storm and wishing one another well. Chung was sitting in a chair in front of his room. I was surprised to see he had on a cone shaped birthday hat. I pointed and laughed, he said, "No New Year for me, American Birthday" and that was exactly right. The only person not present was Dr. Ron, guess he had other plans. Miss. Charlott started counting down the seconds" 10-9-8-7-6-5-4-3-2-1" then she yelled KISS MY ASS, HAPPY NEW YEAR!!!" Martha covered Jolie's ears, I yelled "Charlott! We have a child up here." "OOPS, I'm sorry baby, I forgot myself" she replied covering her mouth to conceal her Cheshire cat grin. This was indeed a happy time, as the beverages finished we got a good laugh as Martha and Jolie banged pots and pans with a big spoon and paraded up and down the corridor. Ten minutes or so passed and we said our good nights, each entering our rooms in turn, closing behind us doors that protect, shield, and keep hidden the strange and painful mysteries of our existence. There was a commonality of feeling grateful and blessed that we made it through another year.

Sometime before dawn there was a terrible racket. The doors of the vestibule were being slammed back and forth against the walls. Then screaming cries and yells for help. "Somebody help me, please!" The cries of horror filled the air, every door in the building swung open. I raced down the stairs in time to see Brick House come flying in and land on the floor. She was screaming and crying, black mascara and ruby red lipstick smeared, stockings torn, blouse ripped. Her bright colored red wig in hand, crawling on all fours toward the nearest corner of the hall. Miss Charlott cautiously cracked her door. Jackson "Crush" Ruiz and his crew came bursting through the vestibule doors. The noise from the garbage trucks was so loud you could barely hear what they were shouting. "You Fuck'in faggot, queer bitch!" He yelled, all the while surrounding Brick House. Each of his crew taking turns kicking and punching, Brick House moaned, screamed, and cried. I figured this to be my last day on earth. I couldn't allow it to continue. I went downstairs, "Leave her alone you animals." There was a blow to the side of my head and I went down. Ruiz shouted "What Doc? Now you decide to grow a pair, for a queer!" He pulled out a Knife and turned to Brick House. "You want to be a bitch, let's make you one!" As he lunged toward her his goons grabbed her arms. Out of nowhere came Chung racing down the steps yelling inaudible words as he banished a long samurai sword. "Yi Yi Yi Yi, Yi Yi Yi Yi! Ruiz and his goons were stunned. They released Brick House and beat it for the door almost knocking one another over. Chung followed, just then we heard a loud thump and the screech of truck wheels.

Miss. Charlott helped me up and we went to the door, Jackson "Crush" Ruiz was lying under the wheels of a garbage truck flat as a pizza. He couldn't have met a more fitting end. All of his crew scattered, not one stayed around out of loyalty. I put my arms around Chung's fragile body and guided him back into the building and sat him on the steps. He looked up at me and whispered "That's that" I patted his shoulder. Miss Charlott who had upon entering proceeded to care for Brick House said, "Doc you better take a look at her." She gave me an all-knowing look, it was obvious Brick House was Dr. Ron, all dressed in drag. Not wanting to embarrass him further we all responded accordingly. "You okay Miss? I'm a … well used to be a doctor, or we can call an ambulance." "No please don't, I'll be fine, thank you." He lifted his wig and stretched it across his head lopsided. "If you could just help me up the stairs, I was on my way to visit a friend, New Year's Eve and all." He tried but failed to manage a smile. Tears ran down his cheeks. We all glanced around, no one let on that we knew the truth. "Okay, sure I'll help" I lifted Brick House up, her arm was around my shoulder and my arm was around her waist. Chung stood with a little difficulty and handed me his sword. Jokingly I said "This would certainly have done the job" Chung smiled and grabbed the banister with both hands. We slowly made our way up the stairs. No one from the building opened a window or made a peep. We just wanted it to all go away and it did.

The police and ambulances stayed out front past daybreak, Ruiz was pronounced dead at the scene without fare of any kind, just gone. A couple of days passed; I was headed down the steps to the hall mail table. Dr. Ron came walking down behind me. When we reached the bottom I said "You missed quite a bit of excitement New Year's Eve" he bowed his head and adjusted he sunglasses that covered a real shiner. Miss Charlott peeped in the hallway. "Yes I was told" he replied. "I hope your friend is alright, she caught quite a beating"

"She's coming along" he paused looked up, as if trying to come clean and removed the sunglasses revealing the shiner. "She's coming along just fine, thank you" he paused again and stared at Charlott and me "Thank you all" he placed his glasses back on and exited the building. As he passed Chung he squeezed Chung's shoulder. Chung looked up unaware of the gesture's meaning. Miss Charlott and I looked at one another. I asked, "He doesn't know does he?" she smiled and replied "Probably not, some things are best left in the dark"

The Brick House never made another appearance, and the incident was never referred to again. It was sometime in January that year we lost Chung. He came out to sit on the stoop and as usual was greeted by Miss Charlott and her offering of tea. The snow was piled high and the slush splashed as cars and trucks whizzed by. This particular morning Chung was a bit on the quiet side, just listening, which of course was fine with Miss Charlott. He sat there staring up at the sky a flock of geese flew overhead, an unusual sight in the city. Chung pointed "Going home" Miss Charlott looked up. "I think they're going south for the winter. They were probably too lazy to get an early start." She laughed, Chung smiled and released the cup. It shattered on the stoop, "Oh Chung" exclaimed Miss Charlott. "You broke the cup" She got up and went to gather the broken pieces of crockery. Chung's arm just dangled at his side. I was upstairs perched on the window seal. "Doc, you better get down here!" Charlott yelled. I got up and started down the stairs, I could hear Dr. Ron lock his door. On approach it was obvious something was drastically wrong; Charlott was on her knees crying and holding Chung's hand surrounded by busted crockery.

She looked up at me tears flowing, I knew he was gone. I knelt down beside her, placed my hand on her shoulder and started picking up bits of the broken cup. Chung's eyes were open and he had a slight smile. He appeared comforted, which made me smile as I closed his eyes. Dr. Ron, Mrs. Martha and Jolie came bouncing down the stairs and off the stoop with morning greetings. Neither of them took notice of Chung's demise, and there wasn't any good reason to inform them at the time. There would be an appropriate time later. Before notifying the authorities Miss Charlott and I just sat there for a while with our friend and family member. I placed my arm around her shoulder and she continued to hold Chung's hand and all was well, Chung, ahead of the rest of us had finally crossed the bridge.

MISCONCEPTION CONCEPTION

(Story Two)

My grandparents on my mother's side migrated from Israel and settled in Crown Heights, Brooklyn, NY. My mother Annie and father

Arthur were both born in Crown Heights, but of vastly different cultures. Granny and grandpa were raised in the Hasidim tradition, however over the years found themselves on the fringe of Orthodox observances and theologies.

If I had to guess, I would attribute it to the fact that while Crown Heights was predominantly comprised of Jewish residents of Hasidim faith. There was also a large Caribbean, African American and Puerto Rican population. We all lived within such close proximity to one another. For the most part we lived a harmonious existence. There were of course disagreements from time to time, but nothing worth noting. Because of religious disciplines the majority of Orthodox residents didn't interact with outsiders, unless absolutely necessary. That said, some of the kids did, mostly those who parents had a more contemporary few of their faith.

My parents Annie and Arthur were friends most of their lives, interacting at playgrounds in their youth and as young adults. In their teens an obvious infatuation grew into a romantic bond and inevitably intimate. Those who surmised or made the assumption didn't approve. As the relationship grew, so did their outward display of affection. Some went as far as to say it was audacious. On my father's side it was no big deal, young love was common, interracial, or otherwise. A few months passed, it was March 1991, my mother began to show, she was pregnant. Granny and Grandpa were outraged. They forbid my mother to have any further contact with my father. According to Granny, abortion was out of the question. The primary reason for terminating a pregnancy in the Hasidim faith is based on the mother's health and wellbeing. The life of the mother supersedes that of the fetus. My grandparents tried to conceal best they could but, somehow word got out, perhaps it was just another summation drawn conclusion, didn't matter the dye was cast.

Neighbors, friends, and family distanced themselves.

My father tried desperately to see my mother; Grandpa wouldn't hear of it. Around the same time my mother started exhibiting unexplained erratic behavior. At first Granny was under the impression she was acting out for being confined to the house. My mother's health got progressively worst, she began not recognizing anyone or being able to control her outbursts, there were also seizures. She became bed-ridden and eventually my mother and I were admitted to Kings County Hospital where she succumbed to an Intracranial aneurysm. That day I was born by Cesarean Section, one month early in August of 1991.

At an early age I was always curious as to why I didn't have real parents, a mother and father. My friends spoke of gatherings with siblings and spending high holy holidays with extended family. All I had was Grandpa and Granny, who raised me with love and kindness, and taught me the ways of a proud people. In all of it I was different, my skin was darker and my hair was kinky. Though the obvious rang loud, acceptance in the community was genuine. My father was a black man. I never met him; it was said throughout the years that he had moved away before I was born. A disparaging word was never spoken, that said, there was never any praise either. Every year the month of my birth was both joyful and solemn. Grandpa referred to August as a lingering wound only faith and patience can heal. One of the darkest months in our community's history, no pun intended. On August 19, 1991, the Hasidim community observers and outsiders of many faiths joined in the home going of a beloved community leader. The procession moderate in length consisted of many motor vehicles and hundreds of walking Hasidim followers. The sidewalks on both sides of the streets were filled with residents paying their respects, some just wanting to get a glimpse. Depending on the point of view of the influencers at the time, you were told one of two versions of the devastating and tragic events which occurred those three days.

The most egregious were committed by would be political hopefuls, agitators and opportunists who characterized the protest as a POGROM perpetuating the myth of a race war. Then came September 11, 2001, America was attacked and we were all brothers and sisters. It was us against them, and that was the new party line. The shock and hurt continues to linger. What everyone craved at the time was simply a bit of normality. Normal never came, just another excuse to hate. I remember Gramps and I sitting in Katz's Deli on East Houston Street. We always shared one of those enormous sandwiches bursting with aromatic, succulent deli meats. Gramps would continually complain about how expensive the food was but we always managed to take home a remaining half sandwich to Granny, not to mention the extra pickles, in a bowl on the table, which he would wrap in several napkins and stuff into his pockets. His rationale for clearing the pickles, he said the restaurant wouldn't have put pickles on the table if we weren't meant to have them all.

During these walks with Gramps, one of my favorite things to do was people watch, studying their clothes and the way they interacted. Little kids being dragged along by their parents always caught my attention. Have you ever noticed when parents walk with their children, they often hold one hand and the child's other hand flaps and waves in the air? If you're close enough, sometimes that flapping hand goes up as if the child is reaching out to make contact. While walking along and passing one another, children have a natural tendency to make eye contact; usually they smile or just stare curiously. While being pulled along, their little heads turn for a last glimpse into what the moment meant or perhaps could have been – maybe the possibility of making a friend.

Skip a few years to the future and I'm 13 years old, just past my bar mitzvah, considered a man by culture and faith. Middle school, where kids regarded me as a wimp, is behind me. I have entered high school, where I'm now an indistinguishable curiosity. Most people don't seem to know what to make of me and sometimes they ask insensitive questions like, "Are you black, brown, a Jewish wanna-be, or what?" Because of past teasing, I've learned enough to look past ignorance. To those who are genuinely curious I just say, smiling, "I'm a mixed Jew." I actually like saying that to watch people's confusion. They step back or look askance, squinting their eyes, and ask, "A mixed Jew?" That's when I explain proudly, "My father's black, my mother's white and my grandparents raised me in the Jewish faith. There, mixed Jew." Some people smile, girls laugh and say, "You're crazy, cute and definitely crazy." I laugh and say, "What do you want? I'm a brown man with a yarmulke." This oddity was sort of my claim to fame. It made me unique. In some ways, being biracial was my bridge. My color gave me acceptance with the black population and my faith allowed the white kids, who were primarily Jewish, to accept me. I guess I lucked out. Otherwise, I was simply a kid wearing a vest sweater, a white shirt, and black pants, with thick eyebrows, who stared at girls, maybe just a little too long, sometimes to the point where I could hear them whisper under their breath, "Little creep." It never really bothered me too much but it would have helped my esteem if it were the pretty girls who noticed me instead of the girls everyone said were old maids. I suppose it didn't matter at that stage of my life. I hadn't ever kissed a girl. I kissed lots of images of girls on magazine pages but never anyone close to real.

One Friday afternoon after school, Gramps asked me to separate some boxes in our attic. "What about Sabbath?" I asked. He cajoled, "Don't be lazy the sun isn't down for hours yet." I saw he knew best so I reluctantly went upstairs, pulled down the squeaky ladder to the attic and climbed up slowly. What a mess, dust was everywhere and my vest and pants became covered in it. Crawling around in the attic wasn't a big deal. My concerns were how disappointed Granny was going to be at my filthy clothes. She liked to wash clothes by hand and always said, "I don't need machines, my mother did it this way, her mother did, now it's my turn."

So, there I was, sorting through boxes, this one over here, that one over there, another one to the garbage. Then, behind all the boxes and hidden out of sight, I saw an old shoebox. My curiosity got the best of me and I opened it. The box was filled with letters, 40 or maybe 50, as far as I could tell. Some had been previously opened and read, others were untouched and neatly stacked. I held one up to the light and then I heard Gramps coming up to check on me so I put the letter down by my side. When he saw the shoebox, he yelled shockingly, "Those don't concern you! They're none of your business, I'll take them!" He frantically started gathering them up. I sat there, stunned. I'd never heard Gramps raise his voice like that to anyone before. It didn't make sense to me. What was so important about those letters? As he climbed down the ladder, I managed to slip the one letter I kept into my pocket. It was wrong but an urgent curiosity overtook me. I had to know. Later that evening, there was a lot of arguing between my grandparents about the letters. They were trying to keep their voices low but occasionally their tones were well above a whisper. I heard my mother's name mentioned several times. I don't speak of my mother often. I've never understood it thoroughly – and I didn't realize that until now, a part of me wanted to keep it a comfortable mystery – but somehow she caused our family to split. My aunt and uncle stopped coming around because of the problem. I was told they have kids, that I have two or more cousins. I can't say I've ever really met them. What is for sure is they're about my age or a bit older. I know that because I've always gotten their hand-me-downs, lightly worn clothing and coats. Through the years, rumors circulated in the neighborhood about kids who mingled with outsiders. Remember, it was the end of a turbulent era, Hip Hop was on the rise and music was loud. Younger people were wild and everyone went to the same schools including non-Orthodox Jews; regardless of their culture they interacted during classes. There was also quite a bit of socializing after school hours. It turned out that my mother was one of the more free-spirited girls. I learned that she was smart, heart- and headstrong and very independent.

Before I was born my mother got what Granny referred to as a brain condition. It would cause her to black out, seizure frequently and eventually die. She died within a year of its discovery. Gramps said that year was an eternity. I often wondered why I didn't end up with my dad. Whenever the subject came up, Gramps' explanation was that my father had a hard time dealing with my mother's illness and just walked away. In the back of my mind, there was always doubt about that story and neither grandparent could ever really look me in the eyes at the rise of my questions. But to use one of Granny's expressions, I sensed "there was something rotten in the herring" and I was going to find out why it was stinking. Finally, all the boxes were sorted and moved in the attic and my work was done. The ladder creaked as I climbed down. Gramps and Granny were seated on the large, lumpy sofa in the living room, both reading, or pretending to be. In retrospect, I'm sure they wanted to avoid discussing the shoebox I discovered. Gramps looked up and asked,

"You all done"

"Yes," I replied.

"Then come and give me a hand, I want to move the television. We still have a few minutes before the sun goes down," he said.

He was proud of that television. We were one of the first families in the neighborhood to have a full screen floor model that displayed color. He worked hard at his job as a foreman in the textile industry and did a special favor for one of his friends, and the friend bestowed the TV in appreciation. Gramps never talked about it but the favor must have been special because no matter how hard Gramps worked at his job, there weren't enough earnings to afford an extravagance like that. The TV had been moved, the sun went down and we had our supper by candlelight. After eating I walked over to Granny and kissed her good night. Gramps pulled me close to him and hugged me, running his large, seemingly baseball glove-sized hand over my wooly locks and whispered, "We love you." He hadn't said that in a while but I was too tired to think about it at length. I was sure there was a good reason behind it. "I love you too, Gramps."

My teeth brushed and pajamas on, I was ready for bed. At the moment I was about to get into bed, my eyes opened wide as if a light turned on in my head. I ran to my bedroom door and shut it quietly. I placed my ear close to the door to make sure no one was coming. As I retrieved the letter from my pants pocket, a warm, flushed feeling came over me. I hesitated. I could feel something was about to happen and nothing would ever be the same again. Backing up toward the bed, I inched my way to the window; there was a bit of light from the streetlamp coming in. My stomach became queasy, I could hear the pounding of my heart and it got louder. As my legs hit the bed, my body collapsed in a seated position and I just stared; I don't know for how long.

The letter was addressed to my mother, Annie Krasbaum, 225 Haraway Place, Brooklyn, New York. The beating of my heart continued to amplify; it seemed to fill the room with noise. I pulled the letter from the envelope and slowly unfolded it. Deep down, I was afraid. The anticipation was actually painful. The last thing I wanted was to discover something negative about my mother, but I had to read it. In a single motion, my arms rose above my head and I fell backward, staring upward toward the ceiling.

The very first line was "My dearest Annie, oh how I miss you." Looking back, I don't know if it was bottled up emotion or the affirmation that my mother really did exist that impacted me. This letter was proof that she was a real person who was cared for and loved. Well, you can imagine how the floodgates to my emotions opened. The letter continued, "I've tried repeatedly to see you. Your father won't have it. He says I've caused enough turmoil and grief. He won't allow me to see you, or my son. Our little mistake, your father says. I've seen Jacob from a distance and he's beautiful. Someday, he'll know who I am and we'll be together. Know that I continue to love you. If circumstances were different, I'd be there at your side." At that point, I couldn't read anymore. My eyes were red with tears and my heart was hurting more than I've ever felt. All I wanted to do was lie down and sleep. All my thoughts at that moment were about what could have been.

The following morning I got up and everything seemed a bit more normal than usual. It could have been that I slept better than I had in a long time because of having uncovered something extraordinary, the truth. Whatever the cause, it put a smile on my face and heart. When I entered the kitchen, both Gramps and Granny were seated at the kitchen table. Granny was sipping coffee from her favorite mug. Gramps teased her because it was actually an odd-shaped bowl with a handle. I sat down and Gramps didn't look up. He just said, "Jacob, have something to eat." He was spreading jam on a piece of toast. Granny got up and retrieved a box of cereal and a container of non-dairy milk. I hadn't spoken a word. Granny sat back down. I was looking at both of them with what I guess was a mischievous smile. My silence caused them to look up at me. I'm sure they could see my glow, feel my sunshine. Gramps asked, "You have something to say?" I got a bowl, shook my head no and began eating cereal. My grandparents' lips were moving but somehow I couldn't hear a thing. All my attention was on the letter in my pocket. I reached over and poured a glass of juice. As I raised the glass to my mouth, I simultaneously placed the letter in the center of the table. "What's this?" Granny asked while sipping from her cup. When she read the name on the envelope and realized what it was and all the implications therein, coffee spewed from her mouth.

Gramps choked on his toast. He just glared as I said nothing and continued to drink my juice. What came next was more or less the reaction I expected from Granny. Waving her finger at Gramps and making other gestures, I didn't know what she was ultimately capable of. "I told you so!" she shouted. "This day was always going to come." Tears were streaming down her face; her arms were waving. "You should have listened! It was always his right! We should have never denied him! You fix this! Make it right! Annie deserves to lay in peace." Granny stormed out of the kitchen, entered their bedroom, and slammed the door.

For a moment I listened to her sobs before turning to Gramps. His head was bowed and he was talking aloud. I couldn't tell if he was speaking to me or talking to himself, or perhaps he was searching his faith for answers where there weren't any. "All my life I've tried to do the very best for this family. Maybe my judgment wasn't sound but no one can say my intentions were not pure." He stood up, tapped his chest, and said, "From in here, I did what I thought was best." He put his hand on my shoulder. "For you, Jacob, and your mother rest her soul. Forgive me." He walked slowly from the kitchen. One thing was certain, the truth was coming. Finally, the big secret, the mystery of my life was soon to be unveiled.

Gramps re-entered the kitchen clutching the shoebox from the previous evening. His walk was more a stagger. He stood there holding the box. His speech was broken and there was hesitation in his voice. I wandered what was most difficult for him, setting the truth free or the box that contained all that was left of my mother, besides, of course me.

"Jacob," he said, "you are now a man. This box and its contents belong to you. It will either make you happy or sad, your heart will tell you which. Your grandmother and I love you. We were only trying to protect you. Forgive us." With these words, he put the box on the table. "Take as much time as you need." He paused and then said, "I think we can put school off this one day." He exited the kitchen. My body trembled with apprehension. I was terrified of the box's contents. I rotated it, studying each side. A half hour passed before I had the courage to remove the lid. Letter after letter, there were similar opening lines: Annie I miss you; Annie I love you; Annie I want us to be a family. Annie, Annie, Annie! All with the return address for Mr. Arthur Daniels, 186 Willoughby Street, Brooklyn, New York.

This was my dad. It was apparent he hadn't run off at all. He was kept away from me and my mother. The letters were dated months and even years apart. There was one letter that pierced my soul like a sharp knife. It was written and received weeks after my mother's passing. This meant he, my father, wasn't aware of her death. He wasn't told! I was more angry and confused than ever. I was overwhelmed by a multitude of unanswered questions. Why wasn't I raised with him? Does he believe my mother is still alive? Was this her choice? Where is he now? I was determined to find the answers myself. I would find him. I looked down at the last letter. It was damp with tears. I didn't realize I'd been crying the entire time.

That afternoon into the evening, I sat at the kitchen table. Granny and Gramps gave me total privacy until I was ready to come out. They heard me push back my chair to stand up because their eyes were fixed on me as I entered the living room. The mind can play strange tricks. As I looked in their direction, they both appeared so small. It was as though I towered over a couple of children who had gotten caught playing with their mom's makeup case. "I'd like to meet my dad," I said. Granny's eyes filled with tears and Gramps just nodded yes. It was a quiet evening. We didn't speak. I stayed in my room re-reading the letters and my grandparents watched that large, flat screen television, which at the moment didn't seem so special.

The next morning, I was up at sunrise. Gramps had gotten up and left the house when it was still dark. I imagined that a combination of pride and shame made it difficult for him to face me. Granny was seated at the table sipping coffee from her over-sized mug. "Good morning, Jacob," she said. "Morning, Granny," I replied. I went to her from behind, resting my hands on her shoulders and kissed the top of her head. She reached up, squeezed my hand, and said, "Have some cereal." After settling into a chair, I inquired why Gramps wasn't home, as he never left at such an early hour. Granny said, "I don't know, he said there was something he had to do and he left." She reached over and squeezed my hand again. "Jacob, please don't judge us too harshly, please." "I don't, Granny, I just want to know, that's all." This time she patted my hand and said, "Thank you." We sat quietly. About twenty minutes passed in silence, despite the sound of cars driving by and kids laughing and talking on their way to school. My attention was focused on the most amazing singing from the birds in our tree out in front of the house. Usually, the chirping sounds were just morning noise. Today, as I listened and paid close attention, it actually sounded like music. There was a distinct calm in the air, a genuine sense of clarity.

Granny and I heard the front door opening and we looked at one another as Gramps entered the kitchen. "Have a cup of coffee," Granny said to Gramps "No time," he replied. "I borrowed Murray's station wagon, it's out front." "And for what did you do that?" Granny asked. "I'm taking Jacob to meet his father," Gramps declared. I couldn't believe my ears. Granny stood frozen yet, pleased at Gramps. Gramps said, "Jacob, get your things, you're going to make a stop before school." I just looked at him in shock. I was happy in my heart at the prospect of finally knowing everything. Who my parents really are, what kind of person my mother was and father is, but more importantly, who I really am. Quickly, I gathered my coat and backpack, kissed Granny and headed for the door. Granny and Gramps exchanged glances with a smile. Just before leaving, he once again looked in her direction and nodded as if to acknowledge that he was doing the right thing. He and I got into the car and slammed the doors.

Murray's station wagon was dated, with lots of dents and a faded forest green color. The wooden side panels were attached to the car by an assortment of shiny and rusted screws. I tossed my backpack over my shoulder to the back seat. As we pulled away from the curb, I reached into my pocket for the envelope with the address and attempted to give it to Gramps, who said, "It's all right, that's no longer the address. He moved some time ago." I asked, "How do you know?" He replied, "I just know, Jacob, I just know." Something didn't feel right. It appeared that Gramps knew a lot more than he was letting on. I sat back and waited for what was going to happen next. The drive wasn't far and didn't take very long. I was, however, surprised that instead of heading south toward the projects, Gramps drove north to Greenpoint. "Why are we going this way?" I asked. "Your father's place is in this neighborhood," Gramps said. My mind was bombarded with so many questions. The street was lined with trees, and beautiful houses. What do I say? What if my father doesn't like me? What if I don't like him? Do I have a choice in whether I stay or not? "OK, here we are. "Gramp's voice brought me back to reality. I had drifted off in thought with a mountain of what-ifs. The car pulled alongside the curb. Gramps pushed open his door. With reluctance and hesitation, I did the same and stepped out. About fifty feet in front of us stood a large house. It was painted gray with white trim and a bright red door. "That's it," Gramps said. He came around the car and put his large hand on my shoulder. "Are you all right, Jacob?" Without looking up, I answered, "Yes." "Good," he said.

We started toward the house. The door opened. A tall man in glasses, a white shirt, a blue tie, and brown pants came out. His attention was focused inside the house and he didn't notice us approaching. Just then, a boy came walking out. The man said, "Arty, don't run." "Dad, I'm gonna be late," the boy replied and broke free. As the boy ran from the house and saw Gramps and me, he shouted with a big grin, "Hey, Jake, what's up buddy? You come to walk me to school?" We slapped hands and embraced so our shoulders met. "You live here?" I asked. "Yeah, that's my Pops. Gotta go or I'll be late. See you at school!" With those words, he ran up the street and a chill ran up my spine.

I turned and looked at Gramps. He and the man standing in the doorway of the house had been staring at one another the whole time. The man had a disapproving expression. Gramps let out a big sigh and once again put his hand on my shoulder. "Come, Jacob, let's get on with it." We walked to within twenty-five feet of the doorway. The man's serious expression began to fade into a smile as he came toward to us. He removed his glasses, revealing eyes glazed over with tears. Taking a deep breath, he said my name, "Jacob." Then he smiled and I smiled in kind. He was my father. Instinctively, he looked over Gramps' shoulder at the car. Gramps lowered his head and said," She isn't here." "Well," my father replied with a pause, "I'd have thought that after all these years there would have been some forgiveness, anything." He looked at me while talking to Gramps. "For Christ's sake, to this day, I can't imagine what it was I did that would compel her to sever all contact with me. Take my son, our son…" My father paused again, sighed, and said, "It doesn't matter, he's here now." Gramps looked like his head was going to explode. He said, "It wasn't her fault and there wasn't anything you did. It was me, my foolish, stubborn beliefs. Annie passed away, not long after Jacob's birth." My father backed up, almost stumbling to the ground. A woman who had been watching the entire exchange from the doorway came rushing over. She was wearing a robe and was half-dressed underneath, wearing slacks and shoes but no blouse. "Art, Art!" she yelled. Directing her anger at Gramps, she shouted, "What did you do?!" As she helped my father to sturdy himself, Gramps calmly said, "I'm doing what I should have done many years ago, which was tell Arthur the truth." The woman looked at my father, then at Gramps. "The truth, the truth about what?" she implored. My father looked up and said, "The truth about Jacob, the boy. He's my son." Backing up a few paces, the woman put her hands up to her face in disbelief and cried, "Your son!"

My father tried to approach her with his hands out but she recoiled. "Don't touch me!" she yelled. "Your son, you already have a son and this isn't him!" Gramps spoke: "Please, I didn't mean to cause you any trouble." The woman stepped forward and shot back, "trouble, you don't know what trouble is. So what do you want for the little mongrel, child support!?" Stunned and hurt, I ran back to the car and pulled the door open. I heard my father yell, "Gloria, shut your mouth.

You don't understand what's happened. I'll explain, for now just please, shut your mouth." He turned to Gramps and said, "Obviously, this isn't the best time." Gramps and my father walked toward the car. Gramps went to the driver's side and my father approached the passenger's side. The window was rolled up and my hand was flat on the glass. My father placed his hand on the window over mine, smiled, nodded, and walked back toward his home. The woman was standing in the pathway with her arms folded to keep her robe closed and looked none too happy.

On the drive back, Gramps and I didn't say much but he could tell there was boiling in my blood and an eruption was coming. I cried out, "She called me a mongrel! Is that what I am?" The car stopped for a traffic light.

"Of course not, Jacob she was angry. I'm certain she didn't mean it."

"It sure sounded like it!" I said.

"Jacob, you're going to need patience. Her world and everything she knows has just been turned upside down. You came into her life like the box of letters came into yours, by surprise. If there's someone to blame, it's me, not them." The sounds of honking horns spurred us to move again. Gramps reached over and touched my shoulder. "If you need time to collect your thoughts, Jacob, we can look past school for one more day. You tell me what you need." I said, "My father called my friend Ace Arty, named after him. Ace is his son and Ace is my brother. We've been friends since second grade. I've decided, I want to go to school today." Gramps said, "Jacob, listen to me. You must be careful about what you say to your friend. It would be wise to wait. I know there are a lot of questions that need to be answered but again, we must be patient. Allow your father to lead the way. We don't know how he's going to explain to his family." I turned to face the window. My heart ached and I felt very anxious, not knowing what to do. Even though Granny and Gramps raised me, I just had to say something.

My eyes swelled with tears; my heart was heavy. I was unsure of what to think or what to say, I blurted out. "I AM my father's family." Gramps didn't respond. I could tell he was hurt and wanted to say something but he just sat there in silence. I didn't know if it was my words that upset him or if he was fully facing what he had done to everyone involved in this estrangement. As we drove along, I knew I wasn't going to be the only one with questions this day.

Gramps dropped me off at school. The day seemed more of a dream than reality. It was as if I were floating above everyone without being seen. There wasn't much of the usual socializing. I did, however, run into Ace – or Arty. He threw his hand up and yelled cheerily, "What's up, Bro?" I held my hand high and our hands met with a solid slapping sound. Little did we know those words would impact us for the remainder of our lives. I continued up the corridor, the words reverberating in my head like the shaking of pennies in a child's piggy bank.

DARK PERSPECTIVES

(Story Three)

Chapter One

Paulino exits the Rockwell Holland Insurance building. The sound of gunfire echoes from within. He gasps for breath, face contorted, body arched in pain as a bullet pierce his side. He stumbles disoriented, dazed, and confused. Pistol in hand, blood seeping through the front and rear of his shirt. He sees three indistinguishable figures coming toward him. He raises his firearm and begins firing. The trio tries to run but are cut down in a flurry of gunshots. Randomly Paulino begins firing, aimlessly in all directions.

Sonny, a black man, exits the municipal building across from Paulino. In an instant he is overwhelmed by the sight and is immediately fired upon. Sonny ducks and takes cover behind parked cars. He pulls a pistol of his own and returns fire. Paulino once again is hit, this time he is mortally wounded. Sonny gets up after a few seconds of silence and walks cautiously into the streets, gun still in his hand. Seeing Paulino laying on the ground, he tucks the gun into his belt.

Bleeding and wounded Paulino tries to speak; he mumbles incoherently. Sonny approaches, and bends down, there is nothing he can do. He hears the words "Myra, forgive me" followed by the piercing sound of sirens in the distance.

Nervous, and fearing for his safety, Sonny attempts to flee. Several police vehicles, including a van arrive, each coming to a screeching halt. Sonny, who hasn't gotten far, turns to face the police who are now out of their vehicles guns drawn and crouched behind the open car doors. Sonny scared and shaking attempts to raise his hands, the police can't see fear in the distance. Suddenly, Sonny hears the word

"Gun!" and steps toward the police cars shaking his head and shouts " No!" He didn't realize the gun he'd stuck in his belt was visible. It's too late, they begin firing. Sonny is hit with a blaze of gunfire and falls to the ground. Several police officers advance, firearms cautiously ready. Sonny lays wounded on the pavement unable to respond. "He's alive!" one officer says checking Sonny's pulse. Another officer stands guard over the two men, gun drawn. "Turn him over and cuff him." barks the officer in charge. Another officer does as he is told.

Numerous emergency vehicles began arriving on the scene. An ambulance attendant races to the aid of the gunshot victims. They began taking neck and wrist pulses to no avail. It appears the only survivor is Paulino who can't speak and Sonny who is alive but receives no medical attention. A medical technician notes Paulino's firearm. It's been hidden from sight, partially by his body. Sonny's firearm lay in the street visible to all after having fallen from his waist. The medical technician stands and begins looking around, surveying the scene. The authorities present at the scene immediately interpret the circumstance as perhaps a robbery gone bad. An officer begins explaining, the technician who is standing listens in. "Whatever the black guy was doing he must have been interrupted and shot the others or they were his intended victims and resisted the attack. The first officers to arrive on the scene see a male black with a gun, victims on the ground and open fire. One two three, end of story.

All who have been listening stand silently nodding in reluctant agreement. The medical technician steps forward. "Excuse me, sorry to interrupt, but your theory doesn't seem to match the physical evidence that I'm seeing. This guy, he points to Paulino has a large caliber gun and looks like he's been shot with two different weapons? One is from a smaller firearm. That one over there, he points to Sonny, the black guy's gun. There, that gun." He turns to the other bodies that are now covered. "All of their wounds were

inflicted with a large weapon. This guy, he points indicating Paulino, he's your shooter. He shot those people. You might want to check out that building." He points in the direction of the Rockwell Holland Building, "there's a blood trail from the entrance. My guess, is whatever happened, started there." The officers look at one another and focus their attention on the medical technician. "You seem pretty sure of yourself." The medical technician replies, "Just a guess, without jumping to conclusion." He shrugs, "Evidence seems to support it." The officers nod. They begin walking toward the HR building, their firearms drawn at the ready. Cautiously, they ascend the steps.

Myra is an attractive woman in her mid-sixties with grey and silver streaks throughout her hair. A kind and welcoming smile, the center piece of a face the years have treated gently. She paces nervously about the kitchen, repeatedly walking back and forth to the window. Every time, parting the flower-patterned curtains. The peaceful street lined with modest homes and trees, a reminder of better times, good times. Presently, the pain of worry and anxiety creases her face. Her eyes glazed over from crying, the faint lines at the corner of her eyes, swollen from rubbing away tears. There's a rustling sound at the front door and shouts of a male's voice. "Mom, Mom!"

"Fredric" she yells, racing from the kitchen to the living room. A young man, in his thirties stands in the center, a crying toddler in his arms. He lifts the crying child up and down in a bouncing motion trying to comfort it to quiet. Myra approaches hurriedly and embraces the man. "Mom what's happened? Where's dad. What's going on?" He looks around anxiously.

"Your father and I were having coffee; he gets a phone call from work and all hell breaks loose. I think they fired him. He went crazy! In all the years, I've never seen him like this. Yelling about his hard work, the years he's dedicated to that company. He was slamming and throwing things. I couldn't calm him down." Myra places her hands over her mouth as if to hide or silence what's to come next. "Fredric, he took his gun from the closet and stormed out! I'm scared. I don't know what to do! He's not answering his phone."

Overwhelmed and agitated Fredric sits the child on the sofa, "Sit here and be still." Reaching for his cell phone with one hand and trying to keep the child steady with the other. "Christ Mom, shit! Did you try calling his job?" "Of course I did." She snaps. "I hope he's not thinking of doing something stupid." After dialing the number and receiving no answer he puts the phone back in his pocket. "No answer. Mom I need you to watch little Paul for a while. I'm going to find dad and put a stop to this before something bad happens." Having seated herself next to her grandson, who is now cuddled in her arms, she asks, "Where's Jessica?" Fredric replies, "Working Ma, she had an important meeting today, I'm watching Paul. Look I have to go. If dad calls, call me immediately! I have to keep trying to reach his office. Dammit! We have enough crap to worry about." With those words and his car keys in hand he starts for the door. Myra offers in a solemn tone. "Be careful Freddie." He smiles nervously, "It's not me that I'm worried about." He exits.

Two women early to mid-twenties relax on a sofa. They laugh and giggle. The elder of the pair, Alicia, holds the tiny fingers of her daughter. The child is learning to walk. Alicia studies the child's balance. "Come on honey, you can do it." She releases the child's hands one at a time. For a brief moment the wobbly little legs hold. Then the baby girl bounces down on her pampered bottom. The two women burst into laughter which causes the child to react

in kind. Mrs. Sarah, Sonny's mother, and grandmother to his baby girl, enters the room. Her silver hair pulled back revealing a wide array of freckles. A tattered apron once belonging to her mother partially conceals a brightly colored day dress. "Why all the commotion, what are you girls doing to that child?" "Nothing Ma, look." The youngest woman, Janice points in the baby's direction "Look Ma, She's laughing"

"Never mind that, has she been fed?"

"Yes Mrs. Sarah, all done." Alicia replies. Alicia and Janice exchange glances and start laughing. Mrs. Sarah turns, "Alright you two, I can see what's going on. I have eyes in the back of my head." The young women continue laughing. Alicia barely able to speak, "Mrs. Sarah, I would not bet against that." Smiling Mrs. Sarah asks, "Darling where is that husband of yours?"

Alicia replies proudly, "You mean your son, the businessman." The women smile in admiration, "Yes, that's the one" Mrs. Sarah with a tickled grin "He got up early and went downtown. Said, he had to check on a permit or something.

" Ma, I am so proud of him." Janice offers, affectionately, "Ever since he graduated high school, he kept saying he was going to own a business and work for himself. Daddy just made it a little easier for him to fulfill his dream."

Mrs. Sarah strolls to the window and parts the curtains. Without turning, says "Bill would be so proud. He and Evans started that copy shop almost forty years ago. Now Sonny is taken up where his father left off. It was only fitting for Evans to sell the shop to Sonny. It's been seven years since Bill's been gone. That place is the only real job that boy has ever had. My only regret is that along with the business, he also inherited his father's gun. Evans said it's for his own protection. Always been a lucky charm. That damn pistol. Prior to having it, there were frequent robberies. After getting it they never had to take it out, not once." Alicia and Janice exchange glances, this time without smile or laughter. "In forty years Bill and Evans never had a problem. Why they kept it, I'll never know." Alicia, who'd been playing with the baby on the floor, looks up. "It's a whole new world out there Mrs. Sarah. People, they don't care who you are. These days, if you have something somebody else wants, they don't think twice about taking your life to get it."

"That's right!" Janice chimes in "These roughnecks don't give a damn. Guns, violence, it's all so senseless."

The two women look at one another nodding. "Girl you watch your mouth!" Mrs. Sarah says sternly, "If there's cussing to be done, I'll do it myself, not you!"

In an apologetic tone Janice speaks. "Sorry Ma, I'm just sayin,' everybody out there has a gun and they're not afraid to use them. You bump into someone, or step on somebody's foot and they're ready to pull it out. I've seen it happen."

Mrs. Sarah shakes her head in response. "Good Lord, where is this world going?"

Alicia tickling her smiling baby says, "You mean, what is this world, coming to?"

Miss Sarah snaps back, "I don't need correcting. I mean exactly what I said, going to, as in down the toilet drain!"

A police officer is posted at the entrance to the Rockwell-Holland building. Two detectives survey the scene, paying particular attention to the blood trail, and conclude that Paulino was indeed wounded before exiting the building. Shot in the back. As they enter the vestibule, to the right lays the body of the uniformed individual, the security guard. A few feet away on the upper landing a woman, faced down, motionless. Her white dress soaked in blood. There are two large holes with black powder burn stains indicating that she was shot at close range. The woman is checked for vital signs. The detective takes a deep breath "Good God! What in hell precipitated this mess?"

Paulino tossed and turned throughout the night. So much so that Myra sat up and asked what the problem was. She could tell from his demeanor earlier that evening there was something serious on his mind. Over many years of marriage she had learned not to push him for answers. When he was ready, in his own time, he would let her know. The sky was cloudy over Beacon, a small quaint town on the banks of the Hudson River, hosting a population of about fifteen thousand people, with more than twenty nationalities represented. It wasn't always that way. The forecast was sun with light showers midafternoon.

Dutchess County and The Hudson Valley once reeked of racism and division. There were riots and multiple protests. Towns were divided and lines weren't crossed. Beacon was once the epic center for hat manufacturing, baby carriages, shower doors and cookie box cartons. Southwestern Dutchess County was once an industrial hub during the fifties and sixties. It fell on hard times and disrepair during the seventies, in the nineties it was rediscovered by an artistic population. It became the backdrop for the motion picture Nobody's Fool starring Paul Newman. That notoriety brought a generation of young people seeking a viable, more economical means of survival. Shortly thereafter was the development of a new arts center, Beacon

Arts Foundation. It occupied the former Nabisco Box Printing Factory. With that the post-industrial slump was lifted and in came the gentrification of Beacon. The economic stimulation and prosperity also had a downside, displacement of lifelong residents. Many of whom were incapable of affording the new high cost of living.

Myra's soft spoken and patient voice called out twice. "Your breakfast and coffee is getting cold" Without any particular ambitions of her own, she had found everything she ever wanted in Paulino. They met in their early twenties. Many who were acquainted with the pair mistook them for siblings. There didn't seem to be a hint of romance. They were more friends in appearance than lovers. That is until Myra got pregnant and began to show. Besides the obvious, their romantic bond began to shine with what the neighbors called, "classic storybook affection".

Paulino enters the kitchen; he is dressed for a day at work with his best shirt and tie; clothing he only wears for important clients, people which he hasn't entertained in some time. As he approaches the table he says "Ah, this looks good." He pulls a chair out. Myra responds, "Hope it's at least still warm." She looks him up and down and says in a teasing manner. "Well, I haven't seen this in a while, big day?" "Not really." He says. "Then who is she?" Myra jokes. Paulino first smiles, then his expression turns serious. "I've had it with that Rockwell Junior." He raises his hand to his forehead while stuffing food in his mouth, barely able to get the words out. "I've had it up to here with that kid. Just got to get in there and show him I can still pull my weight. I'm nobody's charity case." Surprised, Myra asks, "Did he say that? Did he actually call you a charity case? After all you've done for that company. You dedicated your life to those people." "That's what I'm saying" The moment is interrupted by the telephone ringing. "I'll get it. Finish eating."

Myra strolls to the wall cabinets just past the refrigerator. She picks up the receiver and starts pulling the long cord toward the table. "Good morning. Hi Sally, Sure he's right here." Paulino gets up. "It's the office." She whispers. "Alright, I'll take it" she hands Paulino the telephone and exits. He puts the receiver to his ear, "Yeah hello," In an instant Paulino's face flushes beet red. "I'm not staying home! That's my job and I'm coming to work! Well, put him on the phone. I'll tell him myself. Sally, you've known me for the better part of twenty years. I don't deserve this; I have a plan just a little more time. Jesus! What's wrong with him? I'm not going, to let him just kick me to the curb!" Myra has silently come to the kitchen's threshold and has overheard the majority of the one-sided conversation. Her hands gently lay against her heart, literally feeling Paulino's pain. Paulino continues to rant into the telephone. "Sally don't you tell me what's best! You don't know crap! Not even the half of it! I'm on my way and he better be prepared to talk to me!"

Paulino throws the telephone against the wall. Myra jumps and cowers. Myra slowly inches to the telephone and picks it up. Speaking in a low tone Paulino continues his rant "Damned arrogant little bastard." He turns to Myra, "Do you know I once changed his shitty little diapers. His mother had an appointment, there was no one to watch the little snot so his father brought him to work and appointed me babysitter for the day. Granted, I was the youngest employee, probably the least important person present, still he entrusted the care of his new baby boy to me. Now that same sniffling little fucker is trying to throw me out. Well it's not going to happen." He goes to the bedroom closet and grabs an object and stuffs it into his jacket pocket creating an obvious bulge. Having seen this Myra shouts, "What are you doing, stop! Listen, forget about them. We're fine on our own. Paul please, that place, those people. They're not worth it." "I can't!" snaps Paulino. "They have to be dealt with. He heads towards the door. Myra following, "Please, Wait. Paul, please." Paulino exits.

The detectives carefully step over the woman's body and proceed to the upper landing. Blood smeared handprints on both glass doors, evidence indicating that someone tried desperately to escape the violent assault. The wall and sign Rockwell-Holland Insurance Brokers is splattered with blood. Cautious not to disturb the crime scene, the lead detective slowly pushes the right-side door panel open. The leg of a partially hidden body lay behind an adjacent wall preventing the door from opening fully. Both detectives push forcefully, the body slides to one side. As the door opens, the men enter. The expressions on their faces bear witness to the carnage within. With glazed eyes and a choked voice, the lead detective instructs his partner that a team of forensic investigators is warranted immediately.

Fredric walks slowly toward the scene. Police barricades prevent the gathered crowd of spectators from approaching the carnage. He works his way through the crowd to the front. Heart pounding, legs weakened Fredric anxiously reaches out touching the arm of the Policeman standing guard at the barricade. "Excuse me, officer." At the moment of touch the policeman turns rapidly at the ready with a bit of an attitude in his voice. Though his profession dictates witnessing the worst of humanity from time to time, he would rather be doing his usual routine of handing out tickets, strolling through a peaceful morning. Instead, today, he's hurled into a whirlwind of horror that he'll not soon forget. "Yeah, what's on your mind?" Fredric, with a bit of apprehension in his voice, "I need to find out what's going on." The officer is annoyed, "Everyone wants to know, just stay behind the line." Insistent, Fredric speaks in a loud voice which causes the officer to turn prepared for trouble. "You don't understand! I have reason to believe my father's involved." "And why is that?" the officer responds. Looking the officer in the eyes, "because he ran out the house this morning upset. He took his firearm with him." Fredric points toward the building. "He works there, in that building."

The officer looks around frantically. "Don't you move, stay right here." He raises his arm motioning for someone's attention. "Captain, Captain!" He yells, "You need to hear this!" An older officer approaches. Unlike the others he wears a white shirt and black tie. His jacket tailored, his chest is adorned with ribbons of honor and a shiny gold badge. Removing his hat he wipes his brow. In a graveled raspy tone of voice he's acquired over years of hard drinking and smoking, the captain addresses the officer, but his attention is focused on Fredric who cowers to the captain's authoritative stance and arrogant demeanor. "What's this about" he barks to the officer while looking Fredric up and down. The officer prompts Fredric to speak "Go on, tell him what you told me." Fredric hesitates. The officer speaks," He says his father might be the shooter." The captain looks at Fredric and asks for a description. Clearing his throat Fredric hesitantly says, "Sixty-six, silver grey hair, my height, maybe 170 pounds." "That doesn't fit our suspect."

The Captain motions for the officer to remove the barrier to let Fredric through. Placing his hand on Fredric's shoulder he says, "Come with me." They pause for a moment. The captain looks Fredric in the eyes, "Look, there's a victim that matches your father's description. Son this person didn't make it, he was killed." Fredric's legs buckle, the captain takes hold of his arm. "It isn't necessary at this time, but, if you think you're up to taking a look, possibly identifying this person for us? It would really help us out." Fredric regains control of his posture, steadying himself, and says "I'm fine, I need to know." "We'll have to see some I.D. before I take you over there, you understand?" Fredric nods yes, while reaching for his wallet and walking with the Captain. They proceed up the street.

In the distance three bodies can be seen sprawled on the payment. There's a white tarp covering each body. Each tarp is uniquely stained with abstract patterns of blood. Seepage through which the red blotches form unexpected depictions of art. Beautiful yet grotesque images found in the horrors of death and senseless tragedy. Fredric smiles uneasily and is ushered past by the captain. In his peripheral vision he sees another body, the captain notices, and points, "That's our shooter." As they continue Fredric's eyes remain on the corpse. Even covered its apparent the man's hands are cuffed behind his back. The black shiny bald of his crown is visible from under the tarp. They stop between two parked cars. The shoes of the person lying dead are visible, the heels on both shoes worn with thinning soles. Fredric stops, the Captain turns to face him. Staring at the shoes a tear rolls down Fredric cheek. The Captain once again places his hand on Fredric's shoulder. "Are you alright son?" Without looking up, in a somber tone, Fredric responds. "It's him." Kneeling down he lifts his father's exposed arm. Pointing, "Those are his shoes." The captain sighs, "Alright then." He pauses, "I'm sorry for your loss son. Is there anyone I can call for you?"

The two detectives exit the Rockwell-Holland building. They take notice of Fredric kneeling. "Dad, why didn't you just let it go?" The Captain overhears and asks. "Let go of what? What should he have let go of? Son, I know this is a very difficult time, but any information could help us with the investigation." Fredric is suddenly startled by a vibration of his hand and realizes its coming from under the tarp. He lifts the tarp and reaches into his father's pocket. The captain instructs Fredric not to touch the body to avoid disturbing any evidence. "He's my father!" Fredric says raising his voice. He then removes the cell phone from his father's pocket and immediately recognizes the number flashing on the display. He listens as his mother calling out his father's name repeatedly. He mouths the word "Mom" and his eyes fill with tears that trickle down his face. Without answering he disconnects the call. The Captain gently removes the phone from the grieving man's hand using a plastic evidence bag.

The detectives pace back and forth. The Rockwell-Holland building was once a testament to community prosperity, now a symbol of tragedy. They point in various directions and at the tarp covered bodies. Their movements are apparently in effort to recreate the events step by step. Once satisfied the lead detective turns his attention in search of the Captain who is, at the same time, walking Fredric back to the perimeter of the scene. Once Fredric is on the outside of the barricade, the Captain instructs the officer to keep an eye on him explaining that his father was one of the victims. Before stepping away the captain asks, "Are you sure there's no one we can call for you?"

"No, I want to tell my mom in person, I have to get back. Let her know what's happened."

"Sure that's understandable. Just stick around a little longer. There are still a few questions we need answered. We'll be done shortly."

One of the detectives calls out to the Captain. The Captain turns and raises his arm indicating he needs a moment. At the assurance that Fredric is fine he walks to the detectives.

"Hey Mike, what you got? " The annoyed detective addresses the captain in a tone not consistent with respect or regard of rank. "Roy, what we have here is a bloody damned mess! That's what we got!" "Jesus, Mike." The Captain responds. Pointing towards Sonny's body.

The detective, in a frustrated frenzy, tries to speak so only the captain and his partner will hear. "You'll be happy to know, though for whatever reason the black guy had a gun; he didn't cause this!"

"For Christ sake Roy, he wasn't the primary shooter?"

"No, we can bestow that title on that Old Shit over there." He points towards Paulino. "The old man with a hole in his back that he apparently got from the security guard he killed after slaughtering half a dozen people; he's the reason we're sorting this crap!"

The Captain looking over his shoulder says, "For shit's sake Roy, are you sure? I got his kid over there thinking his dad was an unfortunate victim."

The second detective speaks up. "Well, I know one thing; we had better remove those cuffs from the black guy and treat the body with some God damn respect. The press gets ahold of this crap, it blows up in our faces. By the way did anyone bother to check him for identification, or even the possibility of a badge? After all, he was carrying a firearm."

Taking off his cap and rubbing his brow once again, the captain speaks. "Jesus, we really screwed this one up."

Mrs. Sarah, standing in the living room doorway asks Alicia and Janice who are seated on the sofa if they are hungry. Alicia places her finger to her mouth and makes a shushing sound and points to the child that has fallen asleep on her lap. "Young lady don't you shush me. I'll snatch that finger off your hand." "Just don't take the ring finger." Janice says laughing. Mrs. Sarah grins as the two women mimic a high five without touching. "Where is that husband of yours? He sure is taking his sweet time getting back?"

"For Christ sake, get rid of those damn bracelets." The Captain shouts at an officer. The officer hurriedly moves to take off the cuffs. As he touches Sonny's wrist there's movement. He falls back and yells." He's alive!" The detective is quickly on his knees. "Get the cuffs off." The officer fumbles with the keys. "Give me your key!" The detective snatches the key and unlocks the cuffs." Good, now help me roll him over, help me!" As they roll Sonny on his back another moan escapes the unconscious man. "Get a medic over here, we got a live one!" Mike calls out. The Captain moves closer, the officers first to the scene take notice and turns away from the Internal Affairs Investigator that's interviewing them. They also notice all of the activity. The emergency medical technician who made the previous observations work frantically to save what's left of Sonny's life and yells over his shoulder to the detective, "God has a plan for this guy. When I checked earlier, I thought he was gone, dead, no question!"

The Internal Affairs Investigator looks at the officers and asks "You guys seem to have something on your mind. Care to share it or would you rather change your account of the shooting?" The men glance at one another with a bit of trepidation one officer speaks up, "Before we say anything more, we need to speak with our PBA representative." The Internal Affairs Investigator closes his pad and sighs, "I figured you would. "The medical technician working frantically begins to smile. The second of the two, a woman, her blond hair tied up in a bun, bloodied gloves, sweat dripping from her brow, says, "Looks like he's going to make it, he's stabilized."

The Captain smiles, the lead detective takes a deep breath and sighs in relief. He notices a bloodied folded envelope hanging out of sonny's pocket that had been cut away while removing his clothing. He asks for and receives a pair of latex gloves, which he puts on carefully. The envelope is removed, holding it up to the light. "Let's see, what do we have here? "Everyone looks on. As the letter is opened, the detective begins reading to himself. He shakes his head from side to side and raises the letter for all to see. The Captain thrust his head backward removing his cap and says. "Crap! Can this get any worse?" What he holds is a temporary firearm permit." The medical technicians return to doing their job. The detective takes a deep breath and the Captain ponders a plausible story that would bring about a peaceful resolution.

That morning Paulino had arrived at his desk more than an hour early as he'd done for more than forty-five years, despite Sally's warning. He took great pride in always doing his very best, no matter the task. At the age of 18, he was given an opportunity as a delivery clerk at a new start-up insurance company named Rockwell- Holland Brokers. There was a slight brush with the law, a minor offence. An incident which warranted reporting, however, in the small-town community in which he was raised, looking out for one another was everything. The officer, not wanting to taint Paulino's record gave him a swift kick in the pants, literally and sent him on his way with a business card and number to call a friend in need of employees.

Paulino followed through and became one of the hardest working employees and best financial investments the Rockwell-Holland Company had ever made. He was always first to arrive, most often the last to leave. Hard work had finally paid off when Mr. Rockwell himself had taken notice. Soon Paulino was trained in the craft of salesmanship and promoted to salesman. A position he's maintained to the present. He had never advanced; largely due to his inability to adapt to change and grasp the new technologies that were now being used by RHB. He never advanced in position or status he always remained what his co-workers referred to as an irresistible dinosaur.

This particular morning, the day before his sixty-sixth birthday, Paulino awakened in a happy mood. After long resistance he and his wife finally had the dreaded conversation about retirement. He would be eligible in two years, but strategically decided to leave in one. She would have him all to herself. In one year the second mortgage would be paid. He would relieve his son of burden by paying the balance of his tuition, a financial strain that caused friction within Fredric's family.

Watching each of his co-workers file in, one at a time, just one more year he thought. He slowly drank his coffee, one or two people, to his surprise laid envelopes at the corner of his desk and greeted him with a smile and congratulation. Reaching for them with a big smile, it was his assumption they were birthday cards. This delighted Paulino to no end, he didn't think that anyone truly cared. Most of his friends, the old timers, had left or died many, years past. He was the oldest and last of the original staff. Paulino opened the first and began to read. The grimace of his face told of heartache and inner pain. Tossing the first envelope to the side he reaches for the second, nearly ripping the card in two. The blood drained from his face. Taking a deep breath, Paulino stares aimlessly in contemplation. "Retirement Cards" he says to himself. "How could anyone possibly know?" He had only decided the day before and discussed the issue only with his wife. As he sat there a third person came by, this time without a card, just a kind pat on the back; a gesture of acknowledgement. It was the janitor or as Paulino used to say, the custodial engineer.

Adebambo, an aged man of African descent had been with the company nearly as long as Paulino. They were friends for many years. Adebambo means "the crown came with me." Paulino often thought that was truly fitting because his friend carried himself with such dignity and distinction. Paulino nick named him and referred to him in a shortened version. He affectionately called him A.D. Despite his heavy Nigerian accent, Adebambo would always favor Paulino with an untranslatable joke, which Paulino found amusing. "You've been here longer than the rest. It will be hard seeing you go Paul." Looking up, a smile of affection in his eyes, Paulino says, "Don't count me out just yet A.D, there are still a few words to be said." Adebambo smiles in mutual understanding and moves on with his daily duties. Paulino watches as he passes row after row of desks, emptying trash receptacles. Paulino anxiously awaits the arrival of the younger Rockwell. His father, a generous and pleasant man had passed quite a few years earlier. He'd been strict with a penny, but loyal to his faithful employees. He'd given a full week's paid maternity leave to Paulino when Fredric was born. There was no such thing at the time. He treated people with respect and kindness; made them feel as if they were family. Having known and cared dearly for the man, Paulino felt the latter. His son on the other hand was not a chip off the old block.

Back at Mrs. Sarah's house, there's a sudden loud pounding on the front door. The baby is stirred from sleep and wakes crying. Alicia throws up her hands, as the pounding continues. "Ma, can you see what fool is knocking the door down. It better not be Sonny; he knows better than that." Just then a voice outside the door yells. "Sarah, Sarah, open the door." Recognizing the voice of her neighbor Agnes, Mrs. Sarah moves as quickly as her aging legs will allow. "Agnes, what's wrong with you banging on my door like that? You woke the baby!" Miss Agnes pushes past as the door opens and rushes in passing Mrs. Sarah who peeks out the door, taking a quick look in both directions. She closes the door and follows Miss. Agnes into the apartment. Agnes Walters has been a long-time neighbor, friend, confidante, and resident busy body for many years. "Girl, quick" Miss. Agnes continues into the living room, where she ignores Alicia trying to comfort the wakened baby.

At the other end of the sofa Janice has dosed off. With an expression of distaste and an attitude to match, Alicia asks, "What's so important?" Miss. Agnes turns the television on. Janice sits up. Alicia says, "You woke the baby with that racket Miss. Agnes" "Sorry child, haven't y'all been watching the news?" She turns the volume up and steps back. They all stare at the screen. Miss. Agnes, while trying to squeeze on the sofa says, "Some black boy done shot up a whole lotta white folk's downtown and got himself killed." They watch and listen to the television intently. Mrs. Sarah backs up to the sofa and motions for Alicia to hold the baby in her lap to make room for her to sit. "That's probably why Sonny hasn't come home yet. I bet he's in the crowd somewhere watching the excitement.

The newscaster speaks, "We're getting mixed accounts of the shooting. It was first thought that an employee had interrupted a robbery. Now we're told that a disgruntled employee went on a rampage, which could possibly have resulted in the deaths of up to seven individuals and counting." Janice focuses on the television and rises from the sofa, one hand over her mouth, the other pointing toward the television, she screams, "Look, on the stretcher, those sneakers, and pants! That's Sonny Ma, that's Sonny!" She screams tearfully. Mrs. Sarah stands and moves closer to the television set.

"Are you sure girl?" "Oh Lord, what did he do?" Alicia stands, the baby still in her arms she begins moving towards the television hoping against all hope that the man on the stretcher is not Sonny, not her husband. She steps cautiously, Janice crying, Mrs. Sarah moaning, suddenly Alicia turns toward them and says "Hush, we don't know for sure that it's Sonny." Mrs. Sarah asks, "What do you mean?" Alicia continues, "Why would he do something like this? He didn't do anything, listen to me. All of you are just jumping to conclusion, whoever that is, and I pray it is not my husband, he ain't dead. They wouldn't be putting him in the ambulance if he were. You see those other people on the ground, all covered up, they're gone! Now let's act like we believe in the Lord until we find out different. Those shoes and pants don't mean a thing. I'm going to put the baby in the room and then we can talk about what to do." As Alicia leaves the room, Mrs. Sarah moves over to comfort Janice and then holds out her free arm inviting Miss. Agnes to join the circle. "Please God; don't take him away from us." "Amen" says Alicia as she re-enters the room and overhears the prayer. The women hold one another closely as they weep quietly.

Rockwell Jr. enters the building and is greeted by the security guard but does not respond. The beautiful, beveled glass doors with the name Rockwell-Holland etched across the center swing open and everyone snaps to attention. Rockwell Jr. walks past the endless rows of desks. A series of nods and faint good mornings ensue with very little eye contact. Paulino bides time waiting for Rockwell to get settled, his thoughts clear. After a few moments he gets up, cards in hand, and strolls to Rockwell's office, Paulino pauses, and takes a deep breath before entering. He throws the retirement cards on the desk. Rockwell looks up puzzled. "What's this?" he asks. "You tell me!" Paulino responds with more courage than he ever expected. "Why is everybody giving me retirement cards? Is there something you want to tell me?" Rockwell drops his head and sighs, mumbling under his breath, "Shit." "Paul, look, someone jumped the gun. I was going to speak with you regarding this." Rockwell says indicating the cards with a nod. "You've spent the better part of your life here. You still have decent health, look great. The company decided that in your interest, it would be best for you to move on and explore other opportunities. Perhaps, just take it easy and retire; enjoy the rest of your life. You know buddy, have some fun."

"You're the company, and that's not for you to decide." Paulino snaps back angrily. "I have a plan!"

"Look Paul, I apologize for not notifying you of this decision first. I don't know how anyone found out. I really don't have time to discuss this at the moment or get into this with you. What about in a couple of hours? We'll sit down and put this to rest."

"I knew you before you were a twinkle in your parent's eyes. They would be ashamed of this behavior. I know this because I knew them and I respect their memory. Your dad would roll over in his grave if he knew you were doing this."

Indignant the young Rockwell gets up and walks around his desk to confront Paulino. As Rockwell approaches waving his hands, posturing in an intimidating fashion, Paulino backs up, almost cowering, fearing an assault by the younger man. The shouting is heard in the outer offices. A few workers sit up taking notice and listening intently. Still others try to ignore the commotion. "You listen to me old man! I've carried you long enough! You're only here out of respect for my father! Not to mention the generosity of my heart! I promised to keep you around, but that time has passed. The company can no longer carry dead weight. Now, there's a respectable package in place." Rockwell says, taking a deep breath and sighs, "Look Paul, just take the package and move on, please." He walks to the door and pulls it open, his head bowed, trying to avoid eye contact. Paulino slowly moves toward the door. His posture is that of a broken man. Nearing Rockwell he looks up, his lips move, but no sound comes out. As he passes Rockwell mumbles, "I'm sorry, but it has to be this way."

The silence is deafening as Paulino walks back into the main office. He goes directly to his desk, picks up his jacket, drapes it over his arm and heads to the big glass doors. The guard opens the door. Paulino steps through into the vestibule and looks up, the sign Rockwell-Holland Insurance Company appears larger than life. He gives a weak smile to the guard and bows his head. While putting on his jacket, he feels the weight of the gun turns and darts back toward the main office.

Alicia hurriedly races throughout the house. She grabs her sweater draping it over her shoulders. "Where are my shoes?" Alicia says anxiously. Janice sits up on the sofa and removes the shoes from her feet. She and Alicia exchange glances. Janice shrugs her shoulders with an apologetic glance. "Here they are." and tosses them at Alicia's feet, who quickly slips them on. "Ma, I'll call you when I find out what's going on." At the door she takes hold of the knob, pauses, and looks at everyone. "Don't worry. He's fine." She says in a tear choked voice and leaves.

Once downtown, she forces her way through the crowd. "Excuse me, excuse me, pardon, please!" Finally she reaches the barricade and tries to get an officer's attention. He ignores her, Fredric, who has been watching from the opposite side of the barricade waves to the officer. Once getting his attention Fredric points to Alicia. The officer with no option walks over to address Alicia's concerns. "What is it Miss?" he snaps. Alicia takes a step back and says, "Excuse me!" she adjust her tone "I think my husband is being worked on in that ambulance over there. I'd like to get through to see if he's alright?"

"Do you have I.D. Ma'am?"

"Yes I do" she replies.

"Come through, I'll take you to the Captain. I apologize if I was rude. It's been a long morning, please hang on a second" he says accepting her I.D.

Fredric, who has been listening in, makes his way to where Alicia is standing. "It's a good sign that they're working on him. Hope he's one of the lucky ones. My father was also shot, he didn't make it" Tears begin to well up in Fredric's eyes. Alicia places her hand on his shoulder. "I'm so sorry." The officer returns with the Captain. Fredric notices their approach and thanks Alicia for her kind words and steps back. The first officer pulls the barricades forward to allow Alicia passage, as the crowd looks on with curiosity. The captain motions for her to come forward. While checking her credentials he asks, "What's your name Miss?"

"Alicia Thompson." she says. "That identification you're holding belongs to me." He hands the I.D. back. "Yes, it does"

The Captain places his hand on Alicia's arm. She looks down at the gesture and he quickly removes his hand. "Please, walk with me." He steers her to a more secluded area. "Miss, I have some bad news." Alicia stops, puts her hands over her mouth. Eyes closed she asks, "Is he dead? Just tell me! Is he dead?" "No Ma'am, he's not, he was shot pretty bad. He's been taken to the hospital he's going to make it." Knees giving way, Alicia nearly collapses. The Captain grabs her arm and supports her from falling. This time she nods in approval and appreciation at the gesture. "Did they catch the shooter?" She asks looking up into the Captain's eyes, he bows shaking his head from side to side, he mumbles to himself, "Christ" Taking a deep breath he turns to her and fumbles with his wording, "It's a little complicated. The thing is Mrs. Thompson, he pauses, your husband wasn't wounded by the gunman. We're still in the process of sorting this out. Mr. Thompson was wounded by friendly fire." Alicia snaps, "You mean, he was shot by the police!"

"I'm afraid so, in an apparent mistake of identity. We're still piecing it together, exactly what happened. What we do know is that he was present at the scene; and he was armed. I don't mind saying, it's pretty damned fortunate he was. He took down the shooter and probably saved a lot of lives. At the moment that's what we know. I'm sorry."

Alicia raises her hands to her temples in disbelief, "Where's the gunman now?" The captain looks at her, "I shouldn't be telling you this, but under the circumstances. He's dead, we're certain he was also shot by your husband and the security guard, who died of wounds inflicted by the shooter. Before encountering your husband the shooter killed three additional people." We can only assume that Mr. Thompson saw what was happening and shot the assailant or he was fired upon and reacted in self-defense."

"Who was he?" She asks.

The Captain looks in Fredric's direction, "that young man's father was the actual gunman. God help him, he hasn't been told." Alicia once again places her hand over her mouth and sighs, "He thinks his father is a victim." The captain nods. "Yes, if you step to the barricade we'll get an officer to drive you to the hospital" "No, its fine, I'll get there on my own, but thanks." Again the captain nods. "By the way, what I told you, please, stays between us." Alicia responds, "Of course."

As she heads toward the barricade, Fredric remains in wait. Their eyes meet, "Did everything work out? Did they give you the answers you needed?" Alicia looks at Fredric's tear swollen eyes. She puts her arms around him and hugs him gently. "They did, thank you. He's being taken to the hospital, he survived." Fredric sighs with relief. "That's good, real good, I'm happy for you." Alicia releases Fredric but takes hold of his arm and squeezes. "Thank you, my name is Alicia"

"I'm Fredric."

"Stay strong Fredric, I'm sure your father was a good man. Remember the good things. Don't dwell on questions that can't be answered." She pats his hand. "I'll be praying for you."

With those words she pushes her way through the crowd looking back once and disappears as Fredric looks on, his cellphone begins to ring. He reaches into his pocket and looks at the screen which displays a single word, "Mom."

SOMETHING IN COMMON

(Story Four)

Chapter One: The Discovery

Mary and Ivan Provinski have always enjoyed their morning stroll along the back trails of the West Point Foundry Preserve. They walked slowly along the deep ravine. Their early morning constitution doubled as exercise for their cocker spaniel and long-time companion Ralph. Ivan loved to point across the Hudson River then back along the grid iron covered track which was used to roll the huge freshly minted cannons to the Marsh's edge. Pointing he'd say, "That's where they shot the cannon balls!" Ivan would always exclaim as though saying it for the first time. Mary would smile and follow with "Yes, for the North, where the thunder of fire broke the morning calm." Then she would squeeze his arm and touch his cheek all the while looking into his eyes.

Once they arrived at Deer Point, a clear path overlooking the Hudson Highlands, Mary would suggest taking a seat on one of the many tribute benches donated in memory and of loved ones long gone. Her favorite bench was right at the marsh's edge. Ivan, as part of their routine, would loosen Ralph's leash so that he could run free and do the business of purpose and nature. This time spent was special because of opportunity to remind Ivan of beautiful stories from their past. Accounts of love and adventures they'd shared. His diminished capacity having started a couple of years earlier, presenting itself at awkward and embarrassing intervals. Ivan seemingly unaware; Mary painfully of his lapses of memory and the loss of joy, remembrances of their long and loving marriage. Leaning back, hand in hand, Mary places her head on her husband's shoulder. They snuggle up to one another admiring the leaves blowing in the cool crisp breeze of autumn. Ralph is darting in and out of the bush barking at squirrels. Suddenly he yelps. Mary and Ivan look up just in time to see Ralph lose his footing, and tumble down the shallow embankment to the bottom of the ravine.

Alerted Mary stands and urges Ivan to go after the dog. Ivan at a snail's pace cautiously approaches the edge only to be greeted by Ralph who has clawed his way, back to the top. "There, there, that's a good boy." Mud covered and soaked Ralph tries to shake free of debris sending mud everywhere. He then goes shivering to Ivan who notices an item clenched between his teeth. Ivan reaches for it but Ralph refuses to release his find. Ivan reaches again in an attempt to take hold of the object "What do we have here? Did you bring us a present my boy?" Ivan takes hold of Ralph's new possession. Upon the realization of what he holds, Ivan immediately drops the object to the ground. It softly lands a top the colorful pilings of season. Ivan grabs up Ralph and shuffles through the leaves to where Mary waits for him on the bench. He is visibly shaken; Mary must assist him to sit. He hands her the handle of the leash and points a shaking hand in the direction from which he'd just come. Mary nervously walks towards the object. A shiny reflection catches her eye, slowly moving closer she sees a ring and with a screech jumps back as she spots the skeletal remains of a severed hand.

The local authorities launch an investigation. The deceased male was in his mid to late forties according to the findings. His disappearance was posted in the local papers thirty years earlier, during a time in which several young schoolgirls went missing. The last known person to have been seen with the deceased was a man named Leon. His description was average, a family man, wife, two children. At the time, he'd been struggling to make ends meet as a carpenter. The evening of the disappearance Leon, following his usual routine stopped in the local pub. It was payday. He'd have a couple of shots and a beer before heading home to Gloria, his wife. A short stocky round woman with a beautiful face that looked years younger than her actual age, this despite the hardship of raising two children on a modest one salary income. The couple dedicated to one another their life, love, and family, literally the makings of sort after blessings and prayers.

Living about a mile away Donald Faragate, a decent man, employed as an insurance broker. Married and living in a small town, and parents of a twelve-year-old daughter. A year earlier their lives were changed drastically when their daughter failed to return home after school one afternoon. The authorities found no evidence of foul play. She just disappeared, an event that placed an enormous emotional strain on Donald, especially his wife Margaret. Dispirited they experience tension and friction. Through the hardship they managed to remain loyal. Margaret often crying, Donald bitter and angry, however never giving up hope for their daughter's safe return. While doing his weekend chores, cutting the grass, raking the leaves, and listening to Margaret bark additional tasks from inside the house; Donald catches a glimpse of his neighbor across the street removing plastic bags of garbage from the house and hoisting them into the receptacles at the rear. Donald waves hello and spots something yellowish in color on the grass. A container he thinks or some other kind of debris. "You dropped something Bill" he shouts cupping his mouth with both hands for a megaphone effect. Then, with an exaggerated motion, he points to the item with a big smile and watches as his neighbor retrieves the item and stuffs it into one of the bags. After putting the last bag in the receptacle, Bill turns back and waves, mouthing the words "Thank you."

During the next several days both families experience the serenity of normalcy. Leon and Gloria enjoy the weekend with their two children, playing games and cooking in the yard. As the kids run around yelling and shouting Leon and Gloria teasing one another; stealing kisses and touching in intimate ways the kids don't see.

Across town, Margaret prepares lunch in the kitchen while Donald sorts through various forms and organizing work for the week ahead. His hope is that at least three of the possible ten policies will sell. With the television playing in the kitchen, Margaret comes out with several sandwiches on a tray and a glass of iced tea. Her expression is none too happy. As she lays the tray down, Donald looks up. Her eyes are glazed over and he asks, "Are you alright, something on your mind?" "It's happened again!" she blurts out. "What's happened again?" He asks taking several bites from one of the sandwiches. "Another child's gone missing." She says with quiet hysteria. Donald sets the last bite of his sandwich on the plate and stands stretching out his arms to her for comfort. "Let's pray that she's safe. Perhaps she's with friends. Not in harm's way." "It's been days, days!" she responds in frustration. She leaves the relative comfort of his arms and heads back to the kitchen. He watches her leave and returns to his paperwork, stopping every so often to enjoy a bite of sandwich. He pauses to hear the television playing in the kitchen.

Not hearing so much as a peep from Margaret in half an hour. Donald gets up and takes his plate to the kitchen. Margaret sits at the tables eyes transfixed to the screen. Noticing Donald, she begins to rise. "Let me get that for you." She says reaching for the dish in his hands. He motions for her to stay seated. "It's alright, I have it." Placing the dishes in the sink he then turns on the tap and asks over his shoulder, "What are they saying?" In a monotone voice she says, "Same thing, didn't return home from school, hasn't been seen since!" In a sudden burst of frustration, she bangs her fist on the table causing Donald to jump. "How can you be so calm?" "I'm not" he shouts in response to her yelling. Softening his tone, he says, "I just can't let it eat at my gut any longer. It rips me up inside." Totally at a loss for words Margaret raises her hands above her head. "How can it be that no one ever sees anything? Someone must have seen something! A broken twig, disturbed grass, anything! For Heaven's sake, the child was wearing a pink dress and yellow sneakers! How the hell can anyone miss that?" Donald walks over and rubs her shoulders. He, himself feels emotionally battered. "I don't know either, I just don't know."

Gloria and Leon exchange harsh words. Their debate concerns the affordability of an expensive skateboard for their son. "Let's just get it!" Gloria shouts. "All his friends have them. Christ, soon he'll be too old to enjoy one." Leon shoots back. "He'll never be too old, he can wait." With a twinkle in his eyes and half a smile, he says, "I see guys my age riding them. "Really" Gloria says with feigned sarcasm. Leon laughs aloud and puts his arms around her waist. "Alright, we'll get him one. Just remember the money has to come from somewhere and I don't want to hear any complaining later." He lets go of her and turns to leave the room as she gives him a playful slap on the ass. "Why do you put me through this crap?" she asks. Grinning like a Cheshire cat, he continues toward the door and glances back to catch her smiling adoringly. "Moments like this warm my heart," he exits.

Margaret stands at the window, drawing the curtains before heading to bed. As she reaches up to draw the panels together, she notices their neighbor Bill. Continuing to draw the curtains she is hit with a sense of curiosity. "Late to be taking out the garbage don't you think?" Donald pulls his glasses forward to the bridge of his nose. He doesn't look up from his newspaper. "That's for Saturday, not tonight. I've already sorted recycling." "Well, maybe someone ought to tell Bill. Damn fool's out there packing his trunk like he's going to the dump." She says still peering through the drawn curtains. That got Donald's attention, "Really, what time is it?" he asks swinging his legs over the side of the bed. "After ten" she replies as she leaves the window and climbs into bed. Donald sits up Margaret reaches over and turns out the lamp on her side table. Donald turns to her and asks, "The last child that went missing, do you recall what she was wearing?" Fluffing her pillow, Margaret looks at her husband questioningly. "I can't remember it's been awhile. Pink and yellow dress, I think." Donald snaps his fingers, "Yeah that's it, pink dress and yellow shoes." Margaret still trying to get comfortable continues to fuss with her pillow. "Good Lord, what made you think of that?" she asks snuggling the pillow. "Don't know." He pauses. "Funny, it just came to mind." Leaning over he kisses her cheek. "Good night my love" She responds by placing her hand on his thigh without turning. Donald reaches for the lamp, with a click, the room is black. He lies silently, eyes wide open staring into darkness.

Hearing the sound of chirping birds, feeling the brisk cool morning air, Leon stirs in bed. Leaning over he reaches blindly for Gloria. She stands in the middle of the room wrapped in a terrycloth robe. Seeing Leon, she smiles. "Too late, I'm not there. You missed your chance last night and again this morning. Guess you're the early bird that doesn't get the worm. "She teases. "No, you missed the worm." He taunts," but it's never too late, what do you say?" Gloria grabs a towel and throws it in his direction. Leon attempts to shield himself with the sheet. "That ship has sailed mister. Get up. You're gonna be late. Come on, get up! I've got to get the kids up and breakfast started." Without another word, she leaves the room and can be heard banging on a bedroom doors yelling, "Kids, time to get up, let's move it." Leon climbs out of bed, staggers to the large dresser. Leaning forward he looks closely in the mirror at his puffy red eyes while at the same time scratching his crotch. He sticks out his tongue to examine the plaque buildup, yawns, stretches, and heads into the bathroom for a shower.

Showered and shaved Leon enters the kitchen. "Alright, who's ready? "Gloria glances in his direction. "Sit down, what would you like?" "Don't have time." He takes a sip from a cup of coffee Gloria has prepared for herself. "I want to ride with Daddy," says their daughter Sidney. "What about you buddy? Want a lift?" Leon asks his son. David stuffing food in his mouth reaches down and holds up his new skateboard. He has a broad grin on his face, "Got my own transportation right here." Gloria and Leon exchange smiles. Then Gloria points at their son and says, "See, it's paying off already." Leon walks over and gives her a kiss and slap on the butt. "Gross!" Sidney says with an exaggerated frown on her face. They all laugh as Leon walks out. "O.K. Sid let's go," he says, "You too Sport, up and out; and don't be late." As he passes her on the way to the door, Gloria stops Leon and gives him a quick kiss on the head.

As time passed, each day, week and month, a toll was taken on the residents of Phillips Township. There was a dark cloud of suspicion everyone was suspect. A stranger who passes through town often enough to know their habits and routines was out there lurking. What residents feared more than most scenarios, the fiend was one of their own. In all probability it could be a friend, a neighbor or even a relative. No one knew, but Donald, he had a notion. When the disappearances finally came to an end, there was a silent relief, however, the cloud of suspicion lingered. After several years it was acknowledged by all that it was over. Although the mystery was never solved, which meant the killer or kidnapper was still out there. It felt as if the town had been infected by a virus that had run its course and now lay dormant. A festering inner wound waiting for the inevitable trigger. Pure evil, a defect of nature, God only knows.

Chapter Two: Burdened Heart

Donald Faragate, now aging, has considerable health issues. He sits hunched over in an uncomfortable chair at the side of Detective Walsh's desk. The story he came to tell in its second hour. All within earshot are captivated. The desk lamp casting shadows of all against the pea-colored walls. A uniformed officer enters carrying a tray of coffee containers. As he hustles across the room several detectives take cups. He reaches Detective Walsh's desk; the surface is completely covered with files notes and papers. Donald reaches up and is handed a cup. A second cup is placed in front of detective Walsh. As Donald removes the lid and takes loud slurping sips, he is prompted by the detective to get to the point. "The point is…" exclaims Donald, "Everyone was scared! Kids were disappearing and no one had a clue. All those children, my Shirley;" He pauses, taking a deep breath. "We never really found out what happened to her you know. The thought that she might have met the same fate as the others; that she might have suffered, was traumatizing for me, my wife, and the whole family. It wasn't until many years later that she suddenly reappeared. It was like magic. I mean, Margaret opened the front door and there she was, standing on the front lawn, staring at the house. We weren't sure at first. I mean, it was 15 years since we'd last seen her. She was 27, no longer our little girl.

At first there was considerable confusion on her part. She had no idea why the house was so familiar to her. She seemed to know where everything was. Margaret took the young woman's hand and guided her to what can only be described as a shrine in our daughter's memory. Nothing had been disturbed. Everything was intact, including a drinking glass that had been left on her dresser the morning of her disappearance. Strolling around, touching various items, it all started coming back to her. Tears streamed down her cheeks. That's when I knew my baby had come home."

Detective Walsh leans back in his chair and rubs his forehead. "That's all well and good Mr. Faragate, but what has…" proceeding carefully, "I don't mean to minimize the importance of your daughter's return; but how does it tie into the deceased?" The detective felt his patience waning.

"Well early on, when the disappearances first occurred, my wife and I noticed strange, even abnormal behavior from our neighbor. There were strange activities at all hours of the night. Stuffing garbage bags into his car trunk and carting away refuse the evening before collection. Who does that!? Then there was the yellow sneaker that I remember seeing on his lawn. That was part of the description of one of the missing girl's outfit. The last thing I wanted to do was accuse Bill of wrongdoing. So, I just let it be. Then out of the blue it happened again. Another child went missing. The town's reaction was nothing short of panic and fear. Everyone was making accusations, pointing fingers. It was at that point that I brought my suspicions about Bill to the sheriff. He listened, Bill was questioned and released. They hadn't found any evidence linking him to the disappearances." Donald stops and takes another sip of his coffee. "It hadn't mattered; the dye was cast. The stigma of the accusation was enough.

The father of the last child, Leon something, confronted Bill, yelling and crying about his lost daughter, Sidney. It happened at Pete Halden's Pub. Everyone heard about the altercation. Some said there were punches thrown. A few days later the child was found wondering along route nine in the middle of the night. A car slowed for what he thought was a wild animal and saw that it was a child. He quickly rushed her to a nearby diner and called emergency services. Once word got out that she was found safe and unharmed, the town was euphoric. That was some happy day. There were pictures in the papers of the sheriff hoisting the girl in the air like an award, a trophy and the family hugging her. Questions remained, where was the child for several days and who had taken her? Unanswered questions, the fiend was still among us. Even so, the child's return seemed to put Phillips Town once again at ease. Bill on the other hand, tainted, never forgave me. That said, I still had my suspicions. For month's Margaret and I kept a pretty close watch on him when he was home. Years later the bodies were discovered. Had it not been for those children and their dog…ironic, it took children to find the missing. They would never have been found. Who could have imagined. An old forgotten well, three quarters of a mile outside of town near an abandoned hunting lodge, unsealed by the murderer. Poor little dog fell in and drowned before it could be rescued. Once they were able to get to it … Well, that's when the plastic bags were found, at the bottom. So, close, almost a dozen."

Choked up, eyes glazed, Donald coughs. All heads in the room seem to bow with emotion. Detective Walsh pushes Donald's cup closer. "Take a sip Mr. Faragate, why don't we take a short break?." With those words, the detective stood and stretched, everyone in the squad room breathed a sigh of relief. As the officers moved about the room whispering and reflecting on Donald's revelations, Donald walks slowly toward the gated window. Cup in hand he takes another sip of his now tepid coffee. Noticing Donald, Detective Walsh motions to an officer to keep watch. His back to the room facing the window and speaking openly, Donald releases himself of burden, freeing his soul, his conscience. Needing to hear the words said aloud. "I'd do it again." Walsh overhearing the statement motions for everyone to be silent. Donald, with his back to the room, doesn't notice. "Do what Mr. Faragate? What would you do again?" Walsh begins walking toward Donald who has now turned to address the room. "End his life." Donald says with almost a sigh of relief. "Have a seat Mr. Faragate." The detective says pushing a chair forward.

Having finally heard what he suspected, in a calm patient manner Detective Walsh asks Donald to explain exactly what he meant. "We need to be clear about this." Walsh says. Donald smiles, an expression of relief, almost joyful. "I did it. I killed Bill." "How did you do it Mr. Faragate?" "A piece of rope from my garage" Donald rubs both hands over his face. "I strangled him. It wasn't planned, the opportunity just presented itself. I remember the day after the bodies were found. There was a special report on television. The Medical Examiner had all of the bodies laid out. Each bag not half filled. Stainless steel gurneys side by side in a seemingly endless row."

Donald's eyes welled with tears. "On each bag, there was an identifying picture of the child with their name and date of birth. At the foot of the gurney was a pile of clothing last worn by the child the day of their disappearance and that's when I knew for sure. On one of the steel tables there was a single yellow sneaker. On all the others the shoes were paired. At that time, there was a new sheriff running the Police Dept. I reported what I'd discovered again. This time I included my findings from the last report, that report was acknowledged. I was basically dismissed with their gratitude. Bill and I didn't speak for years. I would peek through the curtains and see him mowing his lawn. Whenever he saw me, he'd smile and look away with an expression akin to victory. My gut wouldn't let go. He was guilty and I knew it. Margaret passed a short time later. She always pleaded with me to bury the hatchet and make peace. The only hatchet I wanted to bury was in his back."

Donald pauses, takes a deep breath, and then continues, "It happened on a Saturday evening, recycle night. I was tying up old newspapers and cardboard. I heard a sudden boom, like a wall falling. I ran out of the house and there was Bill, trapped under his garage door. It collapsed on top of him. He was pinned and screaming. His upper body and arms were caught. One was partially severed. His legs were sticking out onto the driveway. I ran over and tried to lift the door, without success. In a strained voice, he screamed out the words, "Inside the button, inside." He continued to whimper in agony. I went into the house, came through the garage and there he lay, helpless. I froze, I couldn't move my legs. He stared up at me and struggled to speak, he said, "Help me dammit! My ribs are crushed." "He passed out I went to him and knelt down. Before I knew it the rope I'd been carrying was around his neck. It was as if I was watching someone else. His eyes bulged bloodshot, and I squeezed until he stopped moving. When it was over, I realized what I'd done. I was kneeling there thinking that this is what he saw reflected in the eyes of that frightened child. I dragged his body into the garage and closed the door. I would dispose of it in the ravine after dark. I didn't know if Bill had a hand in all the deaths; but I was absolutely certain he murdered at least one child." Faragate finished.

Detective Walsh leans back, raising his arms he clasps his hands behind his head, fingers interlocked. Donald leans back as well. "So, where do we go from here, am I under arrest? " "You sure got a pair of brass ones Mr. Faragate" several officers chuckle. "Not for me to decide, we'll leave that to the D.A., I will say this, you came in and admitted guilt to a thirty-year-old unsolved crime; and you had motive! Ordinarily this would be a slam dunk, however there are mitigating circumstances." Donald straightens up. "What do you mean mitigating circumstances?" Walsh begins sifting through the papers on his cluttered desk. Finally, he lifts a file that he'd put there before Donald arrived. "This." He says, holding up the file.

"According to the Medical Examiner, Bill Pulson died of internal bleeding, caused by blunt force trauma to his upper torso. His lungs were punctured by numerous bones. There was also ligature marks around his neck. That, my friend, has been the puzzle until now, not anymore." Relieved Donald says, "So what you're saying is that I didn't kill him." Donald sighs, "All those years of sleepless nights." "No, Mr. Faragate, it appears you didn't. Perhaps it happened when you put the rope around his neck, or who knows, you could have choked the last breath out of him. Anyway, according to this file, your rope was not the cause of death." Donald takes a deep breath, but then Walsh continues, "That said, there is still reason to consider intent and/or depraved indifference, which are charges that could lead to incarceration. Not to mention the unlawful disposal of human remains. Who knows?"

Donald takes a deep breath, as he exhales he buries his face with his open palms. "Then it's not over. What am I facing?" he says looking at Walsh. "I don't know, as I said before. Charges are the business of the DA. We'll just have to wait and see. Right now you're free to leave. Just don't go too far, you know, don't leave town." "Where would I go?" Donald says as he stands up slowly. "I'm a grandfather, two times over. All I have is my daughter and her family. This is it for me. No matter what the outcome. Think I'll just stick around a bit and take my chances. It can't be worse than the years I've suffered internally or what I thought might happen when I confessed." He smiles wryly. "Before you go Mr. Faragate, I do have one more piece of information for you. The Sheriff didn't drop the ball. The case was never closed. If you would have never gone to his aid, the case would have been labeled a tragic accident. The ligature marks are what kept the case open all these years. Prior to his death Bill Pulson was being looked at in connection with the disappearances. In fact, he was about to be charged. Seems your information paid off. Contrary to what you thought, somebody did take a second look. Then out of nowhere he ups and disappears, go figure." Donald smiles, "What do you know about that. Funny, if I'd only listened to Margaret." He starts to leave. "The wheels turn slowly Mr. Faragate, given time and patience, the justice of injustice does actually prevail. Well most the time." Detective Walsh leans back with his palms open indicating emptiness, acknowledging a flaw in the system, a fracture in need of healing. Donald looks over his shoulder and speaks without turning around, with a smile as he exits "I'd like to think so."

THE COMFORT OF OTHERS

(Story Five)

When I heard Vivian was coming to town my heart suddenly filled with anticipation. We hadn't seen one another for at least five years. As I recall we did speak several times on the telephone during the first two years. She had left town abruptly amid a cloud of suspicion and innuendo. I wandered why she hadn't called me personally about her plans to visit. We were after all, or so I thought, close. Instead, like her departure, I had to hear it second hand from Elaine a mutual friend.

Elaine the owner operator of the Moon River Lounge exclaimed "I got news!" before she began there was a barrage of barking orders from behind the bar, she ran a pretty tight ship. It seemed hours before I finally got the whole story. She filled me in on why Vivian had left in the first place and her reason for returning. As it turns out it wasn't just for a visit at all. During the months before her departure, in fact quite some time prior. There was a group of us that met regularly at the Moon River, mostly friends, colleagues, and fair-weather acquaintances. We would rendezvous faithfully every night, drinking, partying, conversation and of course the inevitable argument when the weak of mind fueled by intoxicating drink and illicit fare, bare soul, and truth. Occasionally on what we referred to as a goodnight two to four of us would pair off and disappear for the evening. The next day there was no inquiry or unpleasant innuendo. We respected one another's privacy; it was the unspoken rule. Each of us at one time or the other over the years stepped out and took part in the comfort of others. That's what we called it, primarily because most of us had a significant other at home. This is how we justified our adulterous misdeeds.

The unique feature of the Moon River was that it was our place, a sanctuary not to be shared with spouses. Anyone who violated the code was scolded and risked not being a part of the group. The whole point was not to be on our best behavior. There was a shared chemistry very few would understand. We vowed to be for one another whatever the situation called for. This included mother, brother, sister, lover or just a shoulder to lean on, being there. In the event a spouse did happen to show of course our best behavior was expected. Otherwise the overall would suffer. Which meant not having what we considered selfishly so, a good time. For the sake of continuance, it yielded quite high on the important scale of need.

Vivian and I never left at evening's end that is to say with intentions of fooling around. We'd walk slowly to her apartment, often stopping at some dive for a night cap. Most places were closed at that time in the morning, but for a selected few the doors were always open. After last call and the non-regulars made their departures, blinds would close and black curtains would be drawn. The after-hour drink and illicit goings on began into the early hours of daybreak. Beef steak Peter and Vivian would often stagger out the door together. The ladies called Peter beef steak because he worked out vigorously to keep in shape and it showed. Married with family, he worked as a stagehand. Laid back and quiet, until liquor found him or the other way around. The little snort of coke now and then didn't help any causes. I guess that goes for any of us. After a while, their timing became uncharacteristically early, it also became a topic of discussion behind their backs and reason for concern. The understanding was a little fooling around from time to time to take the edge off was ok. Just as long as things were kept in prospective and no one got serious. In retrospect it seems naïve, we shielded ourselves by claiming we were under the influence and it was all done in fun. However, with these two, something was amiss.

For a couple of weeks, things got back to normal. Everyone seemed to curb their appetite for one another. Peter started making himself scarce, his absence curious but nothing to raise eyebrows. It was assumed he just needed a break from it all. Truth be told, we could all have used a little break. As for making assumptions, well you know what they say about that. Shortly thereafter Vivian started fading away amid rumors concerning pregnancy and divorce. Elaine and Vivian both shut everyone down at the very mention of either. Peter had a family; rules were rules and no matter what had occurred protecting them was paramount. Besides, it was no one's damn business anyway. Vivian resurfaced, barely sipping wine on the occasion leaving earlier and without company. Her being troubled was obvious and it pained me to witness her agony. I'd hope she would reach out to any of us. We allowed her space without prying. She'd reveal in time what she felt we should know.

Several weeks passed, Elaine and I were the last to leave the Moon River Lounge. I asked if she wanted me to stick around and put her in a taxicab. She declined paused and asked me to have a seat. She put her coat down and gave pour to two glasses of twelve-year-old scotch. Elaine confided that some of the rumors were true. Peter and Vivian had indeed allowed themselves to get a bit out of control. The relationship began taking a toll on Peter's marriage and continued to bear wear. Despite the warnings they fell in love, as for pregnancy only time would tell. They say time heals all, well in this case that may very well be true, or let's just say it provides an adequate band-aid. The rumors and whispering ceased, things actually resumed a quality of normality. There were minor differences. Peter played it closer to the vest. His appearances were sporadic. When he did show up, he left early. Noticeably he kept his distance from Vivian. She put on the so-called good face, but it didn't fool anyone. We knew she was hurting. All concerned tried diligently to keep spirits high, more important, heeded the lesson learned. Things never felt completely the same. A tainted cloud lingered, a reminder perhaps.

In a personal effort to keep my friend in spirit and focused, I took up company with Vivian. She and I would walk talk and laugh hysterically at the silliest things. It was nice to have her back and with a smile. Within a couple of months she began to show, it wasn't terribly noticeable. She masked it as she could, not speaking of or making any references. That was actually fine with me. When ready she would let us know. Vivian made the decision to leave town. She did so without notice. It was disappointing, but we do what we must. Not much has changed in her absence. Life continues new friends and acquaintances.

Presently the Moon River appears to be haunted by lean on, hand to hold, gestures of comfort, not only for others, but mostly for ourselves, ghosts lurking in the shadows. Perhaps waiting for closure, answers to unfinished business. Our group disbanded some time ago. I'm guessing with Vivian's return there will be many band-aids removed exposing unhealed wounds. Of course there will also be an inevitable reunion. We were all friends first and foremost. No one would have ever suffered a burden alone. In our odd code of companionship the very least of us was simply to be there for one another, shoulder at the ready.

STOLEN MOMENTS

(Story Six)

Prior to the first moment, I'd seen Jack many times, every weekday morning like clockwork. We both traveled the Staten Island ferry to lower Manhattan. Without ever speaking we would acknowledge one another, a nod or raised chin. I don't ever recall a smile. Seeing the same faces every day the civil gesture was to nod. We did eventually make contact. The terminal on the Staten Island side was always crowded. Under normal circumstances I would pick up a cup of coffee find a quiet corner and wait for the boat to arrive. Not this particular morning, the line for coffee stretched out of the shop and blocked the vending machines. I decided the wait just wasn't worth it. There were only a couple minutes before the boat's arrival.

I approached the main waiting area and realized this was going to take patience, more than usual. Remember, I'd not been able to get my coffee. The announcements informing passengers that the boat had arrived echoed throughout the terminal. The bodies inched toward the doors down the ramp despite the fact that the doors weren't yet open. Didn't matter, the masses begin to push and shove, everyone angling for better position, there weren't any. We were boxed in like animals on the way to slaughter. The doors opened there was a mad rush, everyone trying to claim a seat. I've always been intrigued by the boat. More often than not, I've had to stand because lack of seating. The vessel capacity is thirty-five hundred people, yet there are only fifteen hundred seats. Why is that? What about life jackets, are there enough? Are the amounts calculated in the same way? Is survival based on commuter ability or inability to secure the essential in order to survive? Is there a measure of reasonable expectation for loss of life? An amount considered that outweighs moral responsibility. Boarded I reconciled to standing finding a corner with the hope of elbow room. As I inched my way, squeezing through the crowd there was Jack. He was sitting, occupying two seats, his gym bag in one seat, he in the other. We made eye contact, he smiled nodded and motioned for me to approach. There were of course onlookers who did not approve of his tactics. Many stared discontented. I on the other hand smiled and gladly sat down.

He extended his hand and said, "Jack," I took his hand. He had a firm grip and held tight. "Anthony" I replied, "Most friends call me Tony" "Well which do you prefer?" He asked, "Anthony actually" I said, "Then Anthony Actually it shall be." We both laughed. "Good to finally meet you Anthony." "Likewise" I said, "I find it awkward seeing people every day, acknowledging but never speaking." "Yeah, I know what you mean." There was a soothing calm in his voice, a feeling of familiarity as if we'd known one another for years. He continued talking as my mind was consumed with thought.

His lips were moving, but I wasn't hearing a word. He touched my arm as I heard him say my name. "Anthony you with me" "Yeah, sorry" I replied. He continued talking "Often I play this game of guessing who a person is and what their life is like. Purely speculation, "Oh purely" I responded. "Randomly I choose someone" Jacked looked around, "Say that guy over there, Mr. Cool Breeze" He pointed to a thirtyish gentleman drinking coffee from a thermos. He was wearing an overcoat, open at the front, leather gloves, dark gray suit with matching tie and handkerchief. He also carried a leather satchel that matched his belt and shoes. "What do you think Anthony? Describe his life, remember it's a game. There are no wrong answers. Where is he going, what does he do?" "Okay, let's see. No one wears a suit unless they absolutely have to. I would say he's in business, probably successful, a forward thinker. Well at least enough to know to bring his own coffee." We both laughed.

"What do you see Jack?" Taking a deep breath and a hard look, Jack offered up. "A little flamboyant for finance or law, his bag is hardly worn, doesn't look like it gets much use. More for show than actual work, a wannabe perhaps. Dresses to impress, I'd say he runs with a successful crowd and has need to keep up appearances to blend in.

As for profession, I T tech or mail room supervisor." "Wow! That's some assessment, seriously. I'm impressed" "Don't be" Jack responded. "Been playing this game for a while, remember, there are no wrong answers, Just interesting generalizations, guesses."

At that moment, the whistle of the Andrew Barbari ferry sounded. The Manhattan dock crew was being notified of our approach. Everyone began standing and moving forward anticipating dislodging. Jack was about to stand and I motioned for him to remain seated, he complied. "Are you alright?" He asked. "Sure" I replied, "Just want to wait until the vessel is fully docked. Hard to believe everyone still rushes to the front." Jack looked around "They're just trying to beat the crowd." "Yeah, like ten years ago. Actually on this very same vessel, eleven dead one hundred sixty-five injured, most critically. Pilot error or impairment they said. If passengers had remained seated casualties and injuries would have been minimal. I still get a knot in my gut whenever we're about to dock." As the ferry pulled into the slip Jack asked "Were you on that boat? " "No" I replied, "Two of my closest friends died that day, they were seated together. Another was one of the critically wounded." Jack squeezed my shoulder and offered condolences. "It's been awhile, guess some things stick around as life's lessons. How does the saying go? That which you learn today will help you avoid the pit falls of harsh repetition." As we exited, Jack extended his hand once again. This time there was gentleness, less firm, softness in his grip. "Well, Anthony Actually, I walk from here, good talking to you. See you next time." "Likewise" I replied, we smiled and went our separate ways.

Months passed, Jack and I were getting along nicely. We looked for one another during the week and met at the Terminal Coffee shop before catching the ferry, our standing morning joke was always about the name. "Terminal Coffee, pretty fatalistic don't you think?" "Yeah" I'd crack, "Hope the coffee isn't." Ridiculous but it was always good for a chuckle. Once the weather broke, holiday season behind, trees began to blossom. For the first time other than catching the ferry or meeting for a quick drink after work our social paths never crossed. That is until one day at Silver Lake Park, Staten Island's Green Belt. I was with my wife Grace, our ten-year-old daughter Amanda, and least not forget Leo our overgrown pound puppy whom we were told would not exceed fifteen pounds now weighing in at forty-three. The most gentle and playful, overeating, mountain of crapping creature you would ever want to meet. Over the years he's become an integral member of the family. He's also my most staunch and trusted confidant and ally. I've told him everything and he's never breathed a word.

Jack approached from the Victory Boulevard North entrance to the park. He walked along side and held hands with a beautiful young woman. It seemed he was about to raise his arms to hug, but instead extended his hand to shake. "Hey, hey" he said with a big smile. "This must be Grace and Amanda. Nice to finally put faces to names, I'm Jack. So, whose who?" He directed himself to Amanda who just stood there puzzled. She was very bright and thought Jack was an idiot for not being able to distinguish mother from daughter. "I'm Amanda" she finally said." "Well good to meet you Amanda, Hi Grace heard a lot about you." Grace looked at him and simply replied "Likewise Jack" and smiled. I extended my hand to Jack's lady friend, "Hi I'm Anthony" she reached out and took my hand and also addressed Grace. "Hi, I'm Paula, nice to meet Y' all." She had a distinct drawl. "Let me guess, Louisiana or Georgia?" "Neither" she replied. Jack chimed in "Sorry must have left my manners at home." Paula interrupted, "Wouldn't be the first time." Grace and I exchanged glances. "She's a keeper" Jack followed in response. Raising her left finger Paula retorts, "If I were, there would be a ring on it!" To break the awkward pause I blurted out "I'm afraid she's got you there buddy." We all laughed despite Jack's obvious embarrassment. "I got it, the Carolinas," I said. "Can't hide all that Southern hospitality" Jack said with a smirk. What's up Dude?" I asked. "Nothing much, just enjoying a stroll in the park." "Yeah, really is a great day for a walk." Paula takes notice of Leo lying on his back in an obscene position, Spread eagle for all to see. "Some dog you got there." "Yeah, this here is Leo, My partner in crime and as you can see, absolutely no shame." Everyone laughed. We bid farewell and re-assumed our separate journeys. Once beyond ear shot Grace looked back and said, "That was weird, uncomfortable even." "Sure was" I said. "That one definitely has plans for him." Grace turned and looked at me curiously. She shook her head from side to side. "What!" I exclaimed. "Just some things guys don't get, forget it, not important. Their problem let's not ruin what's left of our afternoon." We continued walking without speaking. Amanda ran ahead, Leo followed at a slow trot.

Monday on the ride into Manhattan Jack and I were having our usual conversations, politics, family, sports. This morning he made a point of telling me how much he appreciated our friendship. What I found particularly curious is that he eluded to my not being judgmental. Truth be told, I honestly had no idea why he would make that distinction. Things being what they are, I assured him the feelings were mutual and I was honored. He smiled and patted my hand as it rested on the bench between us. I must admit his hand remained on top of mine for an uncomfortable length of time. "Hey, I got an idea. Why don't we meet for a drink after work maybe on the island side at about seven o'clock, this way if one of us arrives home earlier we can check in and come back out. We'll meet up at the Yankee Clipper Diner it's only a couple streets from the terminal" "Yeah, sure thing." I replied. The ferry docked and we went about our morning.

At about six forty or so I could see the approaching vessel, it was all lit up in the harbor, a little west of the Statue of Liberty. It's reflection glistening off the river and New York skyline. The view reminded me of post cards and photos tourist text and mail to distant lands, cheap, yet the most valued of souvenirs. Leo and I walked this stretch of Bay Terrace every night overlooking the water. Rain or snow this was our time, for me contemplation and reflection, for Leo, well he just pissed and crapped on anything he fancied, and there I was not far behind to pick it up. A task I've never found pleasure in yet continue. A reminder of my commitment, and of course, who's really in charge. The ferry docked and hordes of passengers began stampeding up the various ramps to waiting buses and taxis. I quickly snatched up Leo no doubt he'd bite someone or get trampled. Jack came out of the terminal and up the ramp. He seemed to take his time, there were signs of stress. His shirt was open at the collar, his tie hung from his jacket pocket. His code of dress was usually impeccable, this evening he looked disheveled.

Upon recognizing me he smiled and waved. Once closer Jack noticed Leo, "What do we have here?" He patted Leo's head. "Sorry Dude has to be done, unfortunately I can't take him in the diner. "No problem" Jack said, "I don't live far, If you wouldn't mind, I'd like to get out of these clothes, maybe have tea instead." "Sounds great" I replied and sat Leo down. We walked along Bay Terrace to the Bay Landing Lofts. "Well this is it, building number three." Jack pointed. "Wow, living pretty large." I said, "Yeah right, I rent, not own." We both laughed. Entering the apartment, Jack pointed to the living room and said, "You can toss your jacket over the back of the sofa, Leo can run free" "Are you sure?" I sat Leo on the floor and Jack made his way to the kitchen. As I took a look around Jack asked if I wanted a shot of scotch mixed in. To which I replied, "Hell to the yes!" he giggled and said, "Then make yourself at home." I continued to look around, there were shelves of books, fine art pieces, beautiful photographs of nature scenes. What I found peculiar, there weren't any photos of Jack or anyone else for that matter. Not even Paula. He exited the kitchen with a cup of tea in each hand, "Chamomile?" I asked, "Good nose, don't forget the single malt" "Yeah the best part" "I've brewed an old college well pot, a small batch." "Makes sense, I replied, why not?" We drank and talked for almost an hour. Leo was turned on his back in the corner, not a care in the world. I told Jack that if I didn't head home Grace would send out the troops to recover my body, any longer I'd better be dead.

We stood and Jack asked for my cup, I asked if I could help with anything, maybe even wash the cups. He smiled and refused my assistance. He took my cup and placed it on the coffee table and stepped closer. He put his arms around me, we embraced, his grip tighten, feeling my arms and torso. He stopped and just leaned his head on my shoulder; his body sort of went limp. For some unexplainable reason I eagerly held tight. His hand drifted south of my waist, it slide across my zipper which caused a reaction. At that moment, my body was pressing against his thigh. Knowing in heart it was totally inappropriate I didn't stop him. This wasn't me, but yet, I closed my eyes and allowed it to continue. I didn't flinch, within seconds I could feel the warmth under my pants. I let out a sigh and took a deep breath. I spun Jack around, my breath warm on his neck, I held him from behind my left arm slid around his throat. I had him in a chokehold, I tighten my grip and Jack gasped. He appeared frightened, "Please" he uttered. I un-did his belt with my right hand and un-zipped his pants, his trousers fell to the floor. To my surprise he wasn't wearing underpants. I held him firmly, it was the first time I'd ever touched another man in this manner I embraced the situation, it felt as if I were floating above watching out of body. I imagined how it must feel, touching, caressing as I'd want someone to treat me. Jack began to moan and grind; I encouraged him he complied with vigor. My hand gripped tighter and I squeezed his throat, he could barely breath. Jack's knees buckled giving way. He sank to the rug and wept; I slid down beside him. He looked up at me, apart from tears there was a smile, peaceful joy. Our hands touched, neither of us said a word. We lay there and dozed half an hour. I jumped up, Jack stirred but didn't wake. Leo was curled at the door, I'm sure instinctively aware of our fate.

My intention was to slip out without disturbing Jack who seemed to be in comforted bliss. As I made my way to the door, I felt my foot sink into a pile of Leo's waste pudding. Vocal reflex got the best of me "Damn it Leo!" Jack awakened startled, one foot in the air I said, "Sorry man, Leo went while we were out" in a daze Jack waved " It's ok, go, I'll take care of it, get home." As I was about to walk out Jack said "Hey" I turned, our eyes met, there was nothing to be said. I nodded in emotional silent acknowledgement as the door closed behind me. On the way home I thought about the evening, particularly about Jack's absence of underwear, his disheveled appearance. Was I played? Had I been the second course of his evenings fill? Silly, for a moment I almost felt cheated upon. I was met at the door by Grace "What the hell happened to you? "I was getting worried, that was the longest walk ever." Graced sniffed the air "Not to mention you smell like shit, stay where you are, take off those shoes and the clothes. I'll get your robe." She placed my shoes on newspaper and stood there waiting for my clothes. Jacket on the rack, sweater shirt, pants. Grace noticed what I'd forgotten, a large wet stain on my underwear.

"What happened couldn't contain yourself!" She threw my clothes at me and darted from the room. "Fucking Ass Hole!" she yelled "Amanda tried to stay awake until you got back, but I see whatever bitch got you off was more important. I really hope she was worth your daughter's happiness; YOU FUCK!" She yelled. "No one got me off, sometimes this happens to guys. We think of a fantasy situation and Boom! There it is" FUCK YOU! "Grace screamed. "Just stay away from me." Grace was really pissed and with good reason, I needed to fix this now. Allowing it to fester would only make things worse. I hated lying but given the circumstance what alternative did I have nothing seemed reasonable. How could I possibly explain what happened? "You'll be happy to know the fantasy was about us, remember the night we dared one another to perform our wildest fantasy. Any act of choice in the car, at the mall. Well, there you have it. I relived the experience, even if it was in my head. It just happened; wish you were there." Grace slowly exited the bedroom with a curious smile "Really?" She slowly came closer "You better not be lying to me" she gently laid her left hand on my chest as her right hand found its way south. Grace planted a big wet sloppy kiss on my lips, more tongue than I had in a while. Just then with the strength of vise grip pliers she reached down and squeezed my genitals. The pain was excruciating, I was at her mercy. "If you're lying to me this will seem like a cake walk." She leaned forward to kiss me but then decided to bite my lip. With a quick twist of her wrist my knees almost gave out. "Is anything left in this thing?" Grace asked with a devilish grin. Without releasing she jerked and tugged guiding me toward the bedroom, the pain was severe. I must admit, the fine line between pain and pleasure was definitely blurred, I was excited.

The weekend passed slowly, Grace and I re-captured a physical closeness we thought was lost after Amanda's birth. I didn't hear from Jack the entire weekend, there was a bit of concern. That said, I figured he would reach out when ready. Perhaps embarrassment played a roll. Personally, I felt no remorse except for lying to Grace. I still can't reconcile why I didn't stop, nip it in the bud instead of allowing it to continue. At that point, the least I imagined was that the stolen moment would impact my relationship with Grace. All said and done, I was actually pleased with the immediate outcome. Monday morning Jack was all smiles and we went about our morning routine without any reference to the encounter. Despite the awkwardness and forced conversation, we both knew the elephant would eventually have to be addressed.

On departure of the ferry, halfway down the ramp I paused and pulled Jack aside. He sensed what was coming, so he headed me off "Dude, its ok, it never happened. I'm good with it, are you?" "Yeah, sure," I replied, "If you're good, no worries then." Jack smiled "No worries Anthony." He patted me on the shoulder "Call you later?" "Sure thing" I responded and watched as he walked away. I was puzzled and very curious the hairs on my neck were on end something was up. I needed to find out what it was. A couple days passed before I heard from Jack, actually it was Paula that reached out to Grace. "Hey Babe, Paula and Jack invited us to dinner at Jack's place this weekend what do I tell them" "Don't know, you interested?" There was a pause "Sure if you are, he's really your friend. I wouldn't mind getting to know Paula a little better." "Alright then, we go. You want to call Paula or should I just confirm with Jack on the ride into Manhattan in the morning?" "No, I'll call Paula since she reached out." Jack and I kept our distance for a few days following the dinner party. When we did finally connect it was at the Yankee Clipper for drinks. After having avoided our elephant for several weeks I decided it was time to talk. Especially since our dinner engagement got awkward.

Paula was in the kitchen putting final touches on dinner. Grace was admiring a series of adventure photographs of Jack and Paula. Seems one or both of them went through effort to give the impression they lived together. The pictures were a new addition. In the photos they appeared to be very serious about the sport and traveled worldwide for the experiences. Grace without turning said with a chuckle. "This all looked like fun until this last photo." She turned and pointed; the picture was of Jack being pushed along in a wheelchair. He had a broken arm and leg. "Yeah, I keep that as a reminder to kind of stay in my own lane. Paula came to the kitchen doorway; she held a large spoon. "That can be a lesson for us all." Paula asked Grace to join her in the kitchen. "Grace" I said, "A glass of wine would be nice, if it's not too much trouble" "No trouble at all" Grace said. Jack stood "Go ahead Grace, I'll fetch the wine. She stood there for a moment not sure of what to make of Jack's movements, he hoisted himself from the sofa and placed a hand on my thigh and squeezed. I noticed Grace's stare, and so did Jack. "You ok buddy" I asked, "Yeah sure thing," He pointed to the picture "Some injuries don't quite heal the way we'd hope." Grace continued into the kitchen. I looked at him sternly in question without speaking. He knew I was pissed and patted my hand which I jerked away. "My Bad" he said apologetically. He fetched the wine. Conversation around the table was totally superficial. The entire evening had an over tone of innuendo and suspicion. Grace knew something was askew and Paula seemed to be aware and chose to ignore it all. I got the distinct impression she had travelled this road before. From the start, her intentions were clear, she had plans for their future. She knew Jack and his ways. Had he confided in her, I wandered. Did she put two and two together and come up with five? Was this some kind of game for them, or was it a power play on her part, a mutual agreement between them that she knew Jack couldn't live up to. Getting us together was the key, like so many times before he would somehow tip his card, exposure is what she was after and he didn't disappoint.

On the walk home Grace and I didn't speak, I reached out for her hand and she refused. It was a beautiful evening along the Bay Terrace, the moon glistened off the bay harbor, the Manhattan skyline in the distance not to mention lady liberty lighting the night's sky. I wanted to explain to her, fill in the blanks. I could see she was hurt the kind that manifest itself deep within the core. You can't pin-point where it originates but, it's there. Like in Rocky III, after he wins his last fight he sits shivering and tells Adrian that something's broken. He doesn't know what it is or where, but he knows it's there.

Grace stopped and turned to me; her eyes were glazed. "What happened back there, did I miss something, is there something between the three of you? I'm not an idiot, something's going on." "Of course you're not." I responded, "It's complicated" "Then explain it to me" she said, "like I'm nine and stupid, like you apparently think I am!" "I don't think you're nine, stupid or an idiot, I can't explain the whys or how comes. It was me and Jack. One night it just happened, I'm guessing it wasn't his first time" "Wait a minute, are you telling me he took advantage of you, were you drugged?" Shaking my head, I knew she would jump to all sorts of conclusions so I just threw it all out there. "No, I wasn't forced. On the contrary, I was a willing participant. I guess, once it started I could have stopped it, but I didn't. We were in the moment; it was instinctively impulsive. It just happened. You've heard the phase, when the wind blows, Yada Yada. It's true! I'm not trying to make excuses. It just happened, some people set out looking for experiences with strictly sexual intentions, female, male doesn't matter. An encounter happens, meaningless. It's like going to the movies, a momentary escape. The consequences rarely come into focus. There's the friendship bonding where men and woman feed off the close exchange of strength from one another. Compassion and understanding from an acquaintance accompanied by a hug. Physical contact, damn it! Grace, I don't know. When you're in need of human contact and someone reaches out, touches you, mentally or physically, there's going to be a reaction. An honest one, what you do with those feelings will determine where you allow them to lead you. I walked a path until I came upon that fork in the road. I would never jeopardize what we have. My life is about our family, nothing is more important."

Grace just stood there, her hands over her mouth looking into my eyes. Her whole body seemed about to burst into laughter. "Are you serious, what kind of FUCKING MUMBO JUMBO is that?" She knew me so well, and I knew her. If I'd come out and just said what actually happened she wouldn't have believed me. So I fabricated a universal truth. "It's the truth, I just felt sorry for him and it happened, but like I said. It's complicated" Grace shook her head "You know life doesn't have to be complicated. If you had explained that at the beginning, I'm sure I would have understood. Not condone, but certainly understood. I know you, the person you are. Try giving me a little credit. You lied. Did Paula know?"

"Hard to say, I imagine she did, wouldn't be surprised if this was all part of her plan." She grabbed my hand "Let's go home, you're an asshole." "Yeah so I've been told. I love…" "I know" she squeezed my hand.

Jack and I continued our usual morning commute, and within a few months he mentioned that Paula and he decided to relocate to New Jersey. Their family was expanding, Paula was expecting. They were looking at houses, besides, he said, a change of scenery wouldn't hurt. We still have a couple things to work through." "I wasn't convinced he believed in what he said.

A year or so later Grace and I ran into Jack and Paula, they were strolling along in Manhattan with a baby carriage. We smiled and waved, pleased to see they were still together. "And who is this little bundle of joy?" Grace said squatting over the carriage. Paula smiled "Allow me to introduce Julie Marie. "She's so beautiful" I said and extended my hand to Jack "Congrats." While Grace and Paula chatted Jack and I stepped to the side. "Nice to see things worked out for you, never figured you would give in to the family thing. Remember, no crumb snatchers or rug rats." We both smiled and laughed "Yeah, I remember. Once I put the ring on her finger after everything, I thought that would be enough, but as you see" He turned to the ladies "We have an understanding, I really do love her we've been through a lot." Paula holding the baby, bouncing up and down as Grace looks on making baby talk. "Julie Marie wanna dance, do Julie Marie wanna dance?" "Hey, she'll never learn anything if you talk to her like that." I said. Grace responded "I had no problem teaching you" "Funny" I replied.

I took a deep breath and once again extended my hand to Jack "Don't get me wrong, I love them both" Jack continued "Couldn't imagine my life without them. Funny the wheels of life will take you in all directions, but it's up to each of us to find our own way home." "Wise words Jack" I wasn't convinced he believed in what he said. You have to want to go home. As Grace and I strolled along we looked back just in time to catch a glimpse of Jack and Paula turning the corner, it was the last we ever saw or heard from them.

FRACTURED SOUL

A fictional enactment

(Story Seven)

Have you ever been to an actual prayer meeting? I'm not talking about just any prayer meeting. Don't get me wrong. All meetings where the lord's name is lifted, is a wonderful thing. I'm talking about an old fashioned Southern Episcopal prayer meeting, a gathering of family and friends for the sake of spiritual rejoicing. A place where hospitality and love overflows, a safe haven. I remember growing up in Harlem, a predominately black community, Wednesday evenings, usually around seven or seven-thirty. A group of about twelve to fifteen neighborhood folk would gather in the under-croft level of Saint Philips Episcopal church for prayer.

These meetings were open to anyone who felt a need. As a child we used to call this space our REC room, short for recreation room. During the week, before five o'clock Pastor Harrison and the custodian Mr. Sonny would set up game tables and a reading section. Some of us boys would run in and offer to assist. The answer was always the same. "Thanks boys, but you all will just hurt yourselves" I'd reply, "Ok Father, I mean Reverend, sorry sir." "It's alright son," he'd say. "You call me whatever you're comfortable with. Just don't call me late for dinner." He would burst into laughter. Mr. Sonny, with his Southern drawl, also had a speech impediment which caused him to repeat everything twice. He'd chuckle and laugh at the same time, "He got you good boy, he got you good boy." I'd smile and say "Yep, he sure did," and walk out. Over the years, I must have heard that same joke a thousand times. The fun was in hearing it told and the reaction it got. It never varied, always the same. This was our after-school session area. We gathered to complete our homework and play for a couple of hours before going home.

Mrs. Gilbert, a tall elderly round woman would start by banging on the piano, or as she called it, the "piana." The woman couldn't play a note. Her heart was in it and that's what mattered. One or two adult church members, volunteers, would always be available to watch us. Truth be told, their real purpose was to make sure we didn't burn the building down. We were a rough bunch, raised right. Very respectful of our elders, why am I telling you this story? Because, in the wake of the recent South Carolina church tragedy, I want you to get a sense of the people that we lost. What they represented to their community and family, the void that now exist in their absence.

At most prayer meetings folks start off at the refreshment table. Hot coffee, homemade muffins, finger sandwiches, you know the drill. Un-apologetic goodie grabbing. After snacking, greeting and a little chit-chat everyone sits around in a large circle. The pastor opens with acknowledging all the new faces. Once introductions are made, what follows is a welcoming in unison by the members. After an hour or so of bible study, prayer and rejoicing the group is asked, by the pastor, if anyone has a loved one or knows of anyone who is in need of prayer. Everyone stands holding hands and individual names are spoken around the circle. The pastor then leads everyone once again, in prayer. Eyes are closed, hands are joined and heads are bowed. Now, I'll ask of you to please, keep that image in mind.

We looked up in shock and disbelief at what was about to happen. I couldn't help but to wonder, why? A faint smile that no one would notice appeared on my face, a nervous reaction perhaps. It was accompanied by thoughts of family members, their faces. It wasn't more than a few seconds before we realized there was nothing to be done. In a moment we would all be gone. The words being spoken were inaudible. For me there was only silence, my attention was on the young man. A young man not any different than any other young man I'd held hands with while praying, except of course, he was white. A young, fractured soul in need of prayer, welcomed into the house of our lord. I, like the others didn't fear death, the reality being we were in the presence of our lord. We were, after all, in his house. He would look after us, there was not to be any physical pain. The real pain was in knowing that once again a member of the flock had slipped through the cracks of humanity. Another of our brethren, a lamb out of the gate, lost to wolves that would bend his mind. Raise him in hatred and release him to prey on his own. Blatant hostility, crimes against humanity perpetrated simply for reasons of difference. The racial divide, that fundamental and proverbial crack in this nation's society, potentially, without mend.

Every person who chooses to believe in cultural cohesion, human equality and democracy have a civic responsibility, a duty to stand, live by example, short of revolution, shout, "No More Enough Is Enough!" and perform that civic duty by simply casting your VOTE.

As the shots rang out, we fell one by one. Our bodies lay heaped in a pile. The blood spilling so much that there was no way of knowing which of us it was coming from. The smell of gunfire filled the air, before leaving he paused to survey the carnage. The door opened and he exited as calmly as he entered. This time there were no open arms. My eyes closed and I like the others was gone.

This story is dedicated to the following

Downtown Charleston South Carolina

Emanuel African Methodist Episcopal Church

June 17th, 2015.

Suzy Jackson Grant,

Ethel Lance

Rev. Dr. DePayne Middleton

Tywanza Sanders

Myra Thompson,

Rev. Daniel Simmons Sr.

Rev. Sharonda Singleton,

Cynthia Hurd

Hon. Rev. Clementa Pinckeny

Un-fractured souls

ABOUT THE AUTHOR

Edward D. Currelley

Edward Currelley is an author, visual artist, and sculptor (assemblages.)   He is a Pushcart Prize Nominee. He's widely anthologized. Publications include HV-MOCA anthologies Between I & Thou; Death is Irrelevant and Through the Eye of the Needle Mom, Egg Review, five Dove Tales International Journals of the Arts, and The Peace Correspondent published by Colgate University and Writing for Peace and in six anthologies published by New Generation Beat Publications. His poem "I America" appears in Split This Rock, as part of their Poems of Resistance, Power & Resilience. His writing has been exhibited at The Hudson Valley Museum of Contemporary Arts as literature inspired by juried artists. He resides in New York City. To learn more visit:

https://www.pw.org/directory/writers/edwardcurrelley

www.ingramcontent.com/pod-product-compliance
Lightning Source LLC
Chambersburg PA
CBHW070653010826
48975CB00013B/1029